A Collection of Poems, Jokes, Short Stories and Personal Memories

P. J. Barsby

A Collection of Poems, Jokes, Short Stories and Personal Memories

P. J. Barsby

First Edition

Published by

imj.com
A division of ISC
2678 Mabry Road
Atlanta GA 30319-2824
USA

http://www.imj.com

A Collection of Poems, Jokes, Short Stories and Personal Memories

Copyright © 1999, 2000 by Percy J. Barsby

First edition, printed 2008

ISBN 978-0-9822355-2-2

United States Library of Congress Number: 2008943169

Written by: P. J. Barsby

Also by P. J. Barsby:

> Byegone Days at Attenborough
> To Make You Smile (A Book of Humour)
> A Humorous Hotch-Potch
> Reflections – A Book of Verse
> Memories – Traditional and Modern Poems
> Goose Fair and Other Poems

Cover art by P. J. Barsby, water-colour, painted in 1931. Digitally enhanced to remove a small water spot and other minor touch-ups.

Edited by: Nicolas Hammond

Printed in the United States of America

Published by
        imj.com
        A division of ISC
        2678 Mabry Road, Atlanta, GA 30319-2824, USA

Dedication:

To Percy's four daughters (Pat, Mollie, Gillian, Paula), eight grand-children (Andrew, Robert, Nicolas, Christopher, Jonathan, Mandy, Alistair, Joanna) and seventeen great grand-children (Kate, Hannah, Oliver, Richard, Dominic, Jack, Harry, Daniel, Amy, Bethany, Alexander, Georgina, Elleyna, Aurora, Aiden, Charles, James)

Acknowledgments:

Many thanks to Michael & Paula Hammond for arranging to copy the Amstrad floppy disks to a modern format.

Table of Contents

P. J. Barsby

Preface

When Percy Barsby died in 2000, he left behind an old (circa 1987) Amstrad computer and several Amstrad floppy disks. These disks could not be read by modern computers and sat in their box for several years until they were recently professionally converted to modern file formats.

This book is a collection of the poems, jokes, short stories, articles, personal memories and one hymn stored on those disks.

Percy was a prolific author and it is unknown if any of these articles have ever been published before.

Editor's Notes:

Where possible, the original text is used, however some editorial changes have been made.

Some of the poems appear twice with similar, but different, words indicating that Percy was not sure which version was better, for example *Jealousy* and *Those Dancing Years*. Both versions are included.

All obvious spelling or grammar mistakes were corrected, for example "abd" when the word "and" was intended; a full stop when a comma was intended. Most likely these were simple typing mistakes that had yet to be corrected. Some corruption of the data occurred because the computer disks were old and could not be fully read. In a couple of instances the words in the middle of a sentence were corrupted and suitable words were chosen.

Some grammar mistakes were left in, usually in a poem as it is believed to be Percy's intent. For example, in *Antique Sale,* the following lines appear:

> That antique was mother's, my one little treasure
> The only thing left that give me much pleasure.

The apostrophe in "mother's" was left in and the word "give" was not changed to "gives".

Most of the poems had titles. For those that had no title, a title was chosen based on the file name. All assigned titles are marked with an asterisk (*). Percy's style was to capitalize the title for all poems – this style was kept.

Some words are no longer in everyday use, for example "coxon" meaning "coxswain". The word "snoodling" probably had a different meaning when *A Bump In The Night* was written. Some words, e.g. burglarism, meaningly are now considered archaic but the original was kept. Where a word is deliberately mis-spelled as part of the story or poem, e.g. "phantasies" in the poem *Alcoholic,* the original is kept. The spelling in phonetical works, e.g. *Gypsy, A Nottingham Monologue* were all kept.

The Romany words in *Gypsy* have all been kept. A "gorgio" is a Gypsy word meaning "non-Gypsy", "matto" is "drunk", "chavi" is "young girl", "chavo" is "young boy", "gavver" is policeman and "dickler" is "sheet". In the original text, Josiah refers to himself as *a young chavi* (young girl), this was corrected to *a young chavo* (young boy).

The original grammar has been kept, even though it may no longer the current style. For example, in *Blackmail* the following sentence appears:

"Who took the photograph?", asked Hague.

The modern style is to remove the comma:

"Who took the photograph?" asked Hague.

In some cases, a question mark was missing, or a comma was in the wrong place. These have all been corrected as was presumed to be a corrupt computer file, or a simple non-intentional mistake.

The spacing in all free form poems, for example *Alchemy* was kept.

Of interest, is that Percy uses his own home telephone number in *The Mirror*. This was left unchanged (the number is no longer valid).

The book is organised into different categories - poems, jokes, limericks, haiku (a form of Japanese poetry), short stories, articles, personal memories and hymns. They were then further organized either alphabetically by title (poems, short stories, articles) or chronologically (personal memories).

All other mistakes are mine.

Nicolas Hammond
Editor

Introduction

Percy Barsby (1906-2000) was a true polymath – he was an accomplished painter, author, journalist and poet.

Percy and his twin brother Harry were born on February 12 in Nottingham. A younger brother Ernest was born a few years later. Percy moved to Attenborough in 1913, living in Elm Avenue and went to Meadow Lane School, Chilwell, until he was 14. He started working at Ericssons for 16/- plus bonus each week. In 1928 he went to work at Armitages in Colwick, riding his bike to work. In 1931, he went to work at the Long Eaton Urban District Council and moved to live there in 1935. He was appointed Deputy Town Clerk of Long Eaton in 1936 and remained in that position until he retired in 1971.

During the war, he was a Report Officer and Billeting Officer (1939-1942) and a member of the Home Guard (1941-1942) before he joined the Royal Air Force and was stationed in India from 1944-1946. Many of his stories and paintings are from his time in India.

Percy moved with his wife, Mabel, back to Attenborough in 1967. She died in 1989.

Percy was always interested in the outdoors. At age 9, Percy and Harry received special permission from Lord Baden-Powell to join the local Scouts – at the time, 11 was the minimum age to join the Scouts.

Percy was a keen swimmer, cyclist and canoeist. He loved all animals and birds and would spend many hours walking round

Attenborough Nature Reserve.

Percy was a committed Christian and very active in Church life. He was a member of the choir for over 80 years and sang in the choir at both Sunday services, carrying the cross at the morning service. He was the secretary of the choir, a bell-ringer, and a member of the Parochial Church Council for over 60 years.

Percy was very interested in journalism. He started keeping a diary when he was 7 and wrote in his diary every day until he died. Unfortunately some of the entries are written in an uncommon form of shorthand. He had over 4,400 news items, articles, poems, letters, jokes, puzzles, limericks, and short stories published in 80 periodicals. Percy wrote under the by-line of Joe Bee, Joe Barsby, P. J. Barsby and Percy Joseph Barsby.

Percy wrote and published 7 books: Byegone Days at Attenborough, To Make You Smile (A Book of Humour) , A Humorous Hotch-Potch and four collections of poetry.

Percy's paintings were exhibited at Royal Institute Summer Salon, London; the United Society of Artists, London; Fitzroy Tavern, London; Nottingham Castle; Derby, Devon, Beeston, Ilkeston, Long Eaton, Romorantin (France) and Southend On Sea.

Percy was an authority on Gypsies and North American Indians.

Over the years Percy belonged to, and was active in, many organizations including:

Attenborough Cricket Club - Vice President
Attenborough Football Club - Vice President
Attenborough Parochial Church Council (for 68 years)

Attenborough St. Mary's Church Choir (for 80 years)
Attenborough Village Bowls Club
Attenborough Village Green Association
Attenborough Village Environment Protection Association
Attenborough Village Hall Committee
Care Group - Enrolment Secretary
Christian Writers
Church Social Committee
Editor of NALGO News, local branch magazine
Electoral Roll Officer
Fellow of Corporation of Secretaries
Institute of Journalists
Long Eaton Operatic Society - patron
Long Eaton Probus Club
Long Eaton Twinning Association
Long Eaton and District Art Club
Long Eaton and District Co-operative Camera Club
Member of the Council (East Midlands Group) Institute of Public Administration
Member of Institute of Journalists
Nottingham Archers
Nottingham Bird Watchers
Nottingham Poetry Society
Nottingham Writer's Club, Editor of Club Magazine

Poems

Some of the poems had no original title and have been assigned one, these are marked with an asterisk (*) next to the title. The poems are arranged in alphabetical order by title.

A CRY FROM THE HEART

I see you each day at the office
and love you so much I could cry.
I'm dying to be your best girl friend
Oh please won't you give me a try.

I may not be glamorous or pretty
and I know that I'm awfully shy
But I've plucked up the courage to ask you
so please won't you give me a try?

I know that I'm not a blonde bombshell.
And men seem to just pass me by
But I'm sure I could make you so happy
if only you'd give me a try.

I'm quite good at cooking and dancing
And could bake you a very nice pie
I'd look after you with devotion
So please say you'll give me a try.

A NOTTINGHAM MONOLOGUE

Well, selt me bob, justarkattit
It's simply peltin daan.
Good job we aint gone aat in it
Weeowt owr coats we'd draan.

Oo, innit cowd, ah'll mend the fire.
Lets evva cuppa tea.
Ta warm uz upp afore we start
Good lor' it's tenta three

Juss put t'kettle on thee obb
Ahll mash up in two shakes.
We may as well ay summat teet
Ahve gorra few nice cakes.

Me owd man's gone t'see th'match
Eee guz wen ee cn get.
Eez gorra seat rait in the stand
So ee doant mind the wet.

Yo know that lad wot lives nexdaw
oo guz aat wee izsen?
They say eez gorra wench in pod
Y'know, that saucy Gwen.

Ahll bet she egged 'in on a bit
Eez sich a quiet lad.
Ahm shaw ee wunnta askt her to
Weeout ee'd gorrit bad.

It luks as though it's baitin naa
So wen yuv ed ya tea
Ahm going daan t'th'market place.
Ja wannta kum we me?

Ahm tekkin Tabby t'th' vet
Thiz summat up wee im.
Eee aint ed owt to eat this wik
Eez gerrin very thin.

6

Ahve gorra bag to tek im in
Juss owd it oppen wide.
Ahll purra peesa flannel in
And lerrim lay inside.

And so we tuk im ta the vet
Oo sed ee warnt too ill
Eed evvta tek it eezy like
And tek a daily pill.

ALCHEMY (1)[1]

On the railway station platform
    I glanced up
  as her male companion
  gave her a fond salute
    on the lips
     and I saw
  for a moment
  the plain face glow
    with beauty

ALCHEMY (2)

I glanced up
as he gave her
a fond salute on the lips;
and I saw
for a moment
the plain face
glow

---

[1] Editor's note: There are two different versions of Alchemy – it is unclear which was intended as the final version.

with beauty.

ALCOHOLIC

Fearful phantasies
ceaselessly swirl in
besotted brain.
Staggering steps on
perambulating pavement.
Reluctant railings
elude frantic fingers.
Reaching, stretching,
reeking, retching,
world won't stay still.
Grumbling, fumbling
capering keyhole.
Lift the latch,
stumble upstairs,
flop into bed.
Never again!
till opening time tomorrow.

ANNIVERSARY

Gnarled finger
in well worn mittens,
lift the blackened kettle
steaming on the hob.

The mantel clock
ticks wheezingly,
like a tired heart
beating out its earthly span.

It is her anniversary,
yet no-one comes to share
the silver teapot,
the best china.

But in her memories
he is sitting there,
opposite her
in the vacant chair.

The years slip back,
the memories revive,
and in the golden silence
the clock alone ticks on.

ANTIQUE SALE *

"What am I bid?" the auctioneer cries
And something inside me turns over and dies.

"Will anyone start with a low thirty five?"
My heart gives a thump, I'm more dead than alive.
"Thirty five I am bid, thirty six, thirty seven".
(They are bidding like wolves for my last bit of heaven).

The bidding continues- I forget there's a crowd
My whole being aching to cry out aloud
"That antique was mother's, my one little treasure
The only thing left that give me much pleasure.
If I'd anything else, I would willingly part
But the sale of that antique is breaking my heart".

"It's gone for a hundred!", the auctioneer cries.
And something inside me turns over - and dies.

P. J. Barsby

APRIL[*]

April - month of frequent showers
Month of brilliant sunlit hours
Frequent changes in the weather
No two days alike together

The First of April is for jokes
which played on unsuspecting folks
are only valid before noon.
For some that time can't come too soon!

April heralds the start of Spring
when new life stirs in everything;
and daffodils and snowdrops bloom
to chase away the winter's gloom.

Of all the twelve months of the year
April brings us the most good cheer.

AUTUMN

Those mellow leaves, so gold and red
that tremble lightly in the breeze;
a blaze of colour, soon will shed.
The Autumn glory of the trees.
Each falling leaf a silent tear
that marks the turning of the year.

There is a sadness in the air.
Those lovely trees will soon be bare.
awaiting winter's icy hand
with snowy mantle on the land.

But this is not a time to weep,
the trees have only gone to sleep

until the coming of the Spring
when comes the great awakening.

AUTUMN LEAVES

Yellow
   leaves
      fall
         ing
        in
      sad
    farewell
  to
    Autumn
       make
         way
      for
    next
  year's
     Spring.

BEREAVED [*]

Mere words bring little comfort when
  bereavement numbs the mind.
A breaking heart heeds not the words
  however soft and kind.
But I sincerely hope and pray
  that time will ease the pain
you suffer now, and by God's grace
  you'll learn to smile again.

We know not why these trials come
  which cause us pain and sorrow.
And though today it's hard to bear,

have faith that in the Morrow
You'll meet your loved one once again
　　so try to feel, dear friend
That though he's left us here on earth
　　his death is not the end.

BEREAVEMENT *

Pain filled my heart, as by the bed
of my dear child, I saw her life
depart.

I was distraught. No word was said
as she lay dead, but then your eyes
I caught.

The look of sympathy you gave
in tear-brimmed eyes, made me realise
I must be brave.

Your sympathy that day, dear friend,
gave me a start, my broken heart
to mend.

BLACKPOOL *

We arrived here on Saturday morning
when the weather was rather cool
but became very hot on the Sunday
so we went for a swim in the pool.
There is plenty to do and enjoy here
The Pleasure Beach on the South Shore
with roundabouts, chair-o-planes, water sports
and coconut shies and lots more.

On the North Shore the Blackpool Tower
with breath taking views from the top
is the venue for fabulous dance bands
and dancing that's almost non-stop.
Yes, there's plenty to do while in Blackpool
A place that is full of good cheer.
So I'll close with that well known greeting
From both of us - WISH YOU WERE HERE.

BLOOD SPORT

The spiteful crack of a gun,
reverberating in the hills,
shatters the calm
of a summer evening.

Wildfowl scatter in alarm
swimming and scuttering
to safety.

Except one.

Feathers flutter,
body contorts
in frenzied pain until
the struggle for life
is over.

The man picks up
the still warm body.
Tramps home content
to wife and supper.

Leaving hungry fledgelings
waiting in vain
for their evening meal.

P. J. Barsby

BONFIRE NIGHT

The sparkler gives a fairy light
in the darkness of the night.
A catherine wheel fixed to a post
gives shimmering shower and then is lost.
While whizzing rockets in the sky
send coloured clusters from on high.

Then from the bonfire comes a scream,
a child with clothes alight is seen
running about in maddening pain.
her shrill screams come again, again.

The flames are smothered, doctor called.
The sobbing child, now partially bald,
is rushed to hospital, her plight
is desperate to save her sight.

Surely, surely the time has come
to give up fireworks at home,
and take the children after dark
to see the fireworks on the park.

While fire is generally a friend,
with warmth and comfort at its end;
we should be careful in its use
and teach the children not to abuse.

BOYHOOD DREAM COMES TRUE

I was just a little school-boy
When I first read Hiawatha.
All about American Indians
As they lived in splendid freedom.
I was haunted by the poem
By the rhythm of the poem

14

By the free life of the Indian
By his living close to nature.
And my heart had one ambition.
To learn more about the red man.
And I made a vow that one day
I would see these once proud Indians
In their homes among the Rockies.
In their present Reservations.

Forty summers came and went by.
Forty winters while I waited
Till I had sufficient money
To achieve my life's ambition.
Then I flew from Heathrow Airport
Flew from London to Montreal
To the great Canadian city.
There I took the iron monster
To the mountains and the prairies
Where the buffalo in their thousand
Roamed the plains in days gone by.
Hunted nobly by the Indians
Slain in thousands by the white man.

As the iron horse sped westward
Through the woodlands of Ontario
And the plains of Manitoba.
Through the prairies of Saskatchewan
And the rangelands of Alberta
To the foothills of the Rockies
I looked out for signs of Indians.
Saw the Blackfeet Reservation
And the Stoney lands at Morley
Passed through towns with names redolent
Of the glamour of the old West
Moose Jaw, Red Deer, Temiskaming

P. J. Barsby

Swift Current and Medicine Hat
Then I reached the Rocky Mountains
Eagerly looked out for Indians
Met a family of Stoneys
At the Indian Trading Post.

They were dressed in white man's clothing
Cowboy hats, check shirts, and trousers.
And the women wore long dresses
Of a bygone age and fashion.
But the women, men and children
All were wearing beaded footwear.

Here I met an Indian chieftain
Dressed in fringed and beaded buckskin.
On his head a feathered head-dress
With a decorated headband
And beaded discs on either side.
Where the nodding eagle feathers
Crowned with fluffies, tipped with horsehair
Trailed in a descending cascade
Down his back and to his ankles.
In his hand he held a tomahawk
Gay with feathers like a peace pipe.
On his feet were beaded moccasins
And a sheath knife in his hip belt
His Indian name was Two Young Man.

He was over eighty summers.
Proud he looked, though with a sadness
On his copper-coloured features.
He had been a mediator
For the Army in the old days.
Now received a Government pension,
Lived on Morley Reservation

Where he did a little farming,
Raising horses, growing food crops.
And his squaw did beaded craftwork
Which she sold to make a living.
And this once proud Indian chieftain
Told me of their past existence.
How, before the white man entered
On to their ancestral prairies
They had lived the life of true men.
Lived a life as free as eagles.

In their boyhood and their manhood
They were taught the art of living
Taught the arts of war and hunting
And the gambling games of winter.
They were matchless in their courage
In their bravery and endurance.
In their knowledge of all wild things
In their unity with nature.

Very picturesque their lives were
Dressed in fringed and beaded buckskins
And the noble feathered head-dress
Worn by chiefs and other sachems.
Cosy were their stately teepees
Warm in winter, cool in summer
Soon erected, soon dismantled
In their nomadic existence.
And he told me, in the old days
Men had taken part in raiding
Other tribes to steal their horses
Counting coup for each horse stolen.
Older warriors had told him
Of their fighting with the white man
Of their bravery and courage

To protect their homes and children.
Ah, no more such noble warriors
Could be found on earth as they were.
Now the tribes have no incentive
Living on the Reservations
Eking out a poor existence
On the pitiful allowance
Handed to them by the Government
As recompense for land they ceded
Under treaties long forgotten.
Treaties broken by the white man
Always honoured by the Indians
In those far off, tragic decades.
Now the Indians are encouraged
To regain their once proud spirit
And retain their crafts and customs.
Once again be self-reliant
And a credit to the nation.
So perhaps in future decades
They will gain their rightful status
As a well-respected people
In the land they owned and fought for.

CANOEING *

Silently we drift downstream
on the placid water, our progress
scarcely causing a ripple.
A water vole,
emerging from its nest on the river bank,
swims across the slow-moving water,
ignoring our approach.

The light paddle,
leisurely dipped into the water,

guides us through the arch of the bridge,
where the tributary joins the main river.
Here, a pair of swans
proudly accompany their brood of cygnets,
quietly calling them from straying
as we pass.

The setting sun
lights up the houseboats
along the bank; casting shadows
across the meadow.
Everywhere there is peace and quiet,
time to contemplate
the beauty of nature,
the joy of travel by canoe.
No noise. no smell of petrol,
no diesel fumes,
no carbon dioxide
from countless exhausts.

We return from our journey
refreshed, and at peace with the world.

CHILDREN PLAYING *

From the playground
came the sound
of children at play.
Shrill cries, bright eyes,
Shouting, laughing,
enjoying the fray.
Memories revived
of a small boy,
playing those games
with zest and joy.

And I mused on the years
that had passed since then;
the sadness in the world,
and wished again
that I could recapture,
if only for a day,
the innocent happiness
of children at play.

CHRISTMAS EVE

It was Christmas Eve at the Horse and Groom
And some of us sat in the pub's best room
There was Frankie and Tom and 'Podgy' and 'Slim'
And Freddie and Albert and George and Jim
And Millie the barmaid, a buxom lass
Who didn't mind customers making a pass.

"Let's all do a turn", suggested young Fred
"And each put in kitty a pound a head.
Then the one who's turn is voted the best
Will collect the money from all the rest.
And Millie the barmaid, the one that's so pretty
Will act as the judge and hold the kitty

We had 'Sweet Nellie Dean' that well known pub 'hymn'
And a comic duet by Podgy and Slim.
Then drumming by George who is in a dance band
And Frankie amazed us with his sleight of hand.

Then Tom took his shirt off exposing his chest
Which was covered with hair like a dirty brown vest.
And shouting "Me Tarzan" he grabbed hold of Millie
And the rest of us thought he was just being silly.

But Millie enjoyed being squeezed to his chest
And when released voted 'Tarzan' the best.
We were somewhat consoled when Tom said with a grin
"Drinks are on the house, lads, so get fell in!"

CHRISTMAS SHOPPING

Christmas shopping with the wife
Missing football, what a life
Window gazing, every shop
Standing till I'm fit to drop.

"Look at this" and "Look at that"
"Hello, Brenda - stop for chat.
Tramping here and tramping there
Jostling crowds are everywhere.

As we go into each shop
I hope the purchasing will stop
We've now got carrier bags galore
Each advertising someone's store

At the next shop, purchase tights
"and we need some fairy lights.
If we buy a Christmas tree
We'll get the fairy lights free".

Carrying the tree, I feel a chump
Can you wonder I've got the hump.
Fingers ache and feeling sore
I just can't carry any more.

At last arrive home, rest my feet
With slippers on, it's quite a treat.
My wife looks up from paper, says
"The sales are on in a few days".

New Year bargains! Not on your nelly
I'll stay at home and watch the telly!

CIGARETTE CARD MAN [*]

Every Friday,
we would meet him
(my brother and I)
on the footpath
across the ploughed field
on the way to school.

A genial man,
turned down floppy hat,
long jacket
knee bagged trousers
heavy boots
and the slow
unhurried movements
of a man of the soil.
(He was, in fact, a gardener).

He would stop and give us
clean cigarette cards
from a fresh packet
of Gold-Flake.
The cards were a series
of British Wild Birds,
with the pungent odour
of the tobacco on them.

We called him
The Cigarette Card Man.
Left school and
never saw him again.

Strange how, after fifty years
we remember his kindness
and the fragrant smell
of his tobacco,
though we can't recall
his face.

DISTORTING MIRROR *

The face
reflected in the mirror
is surely distorted.
Too prominent nose
staring eyes,
sickly grin
showing uneven teeth
like a snarl.
Is that reflection
really me? No.
Thank goodness, it's
a distorting mirror.
Or is it?
Is that how my friends
see me,
or is the mirror
telling me something
I ought to know?
Subdued,
I turn away.

FIRST NIGHT

A calm air concealing unwonted excitement.
Pleasant anticipation of an evening out.
My lady in her boudoir with hairbrush and comb
Emerges much later looking chic and well-groomed.

Both husband and wife look their best, but self conscious
As they take their stall seats in the dimly lit hall.
A rustle of programmes, and bright subdued chatter
As the strumming and scraping of fiddles begin.

Excitement wells up as the overture is played.
The theatre lights dim and the plush curtains part
To reveal the rich setting of the opening act
As the audience sits back with an air of content.

There's nothing quite like the first night of a new play
An air of excitement can distinctly be felt.
The fate of the play is in the lap of the gods.
And the audience for one night themselves are the gods.

FLAKED FLINT *

I see him now
squatting on skin clad haunches;
stone hammer rising and falling
with rhythmic regularity.

Was he a skilled craftsman,
good hunter,
father of a family,
or a young man as yet unskilled?

The work he dropped
maybe three thousand years ago
lies in my hand.
A knapped and flaked flint
picked up at random
from pebbles in puddled water.

Who was this knapper
whose hand I cannot grasp
but whose discarded work
lies in my palm,
bridging time past

I slip the flint into my pocket,
and continue my journey
but now I am not alone. In my thoughts
a stone age companion accompanies me.

GOOSE FAIR

Loud blare of music
on the still night air.
Pungent odour of
hotdogs and wet grass.
Merry jostling crowds
mingling here and there
in the narrow alleys,
trying to pass
between brightly lit stalls
of coconut shies
and jet-dancing balls.

The Tunnel of Love
with its thrills and joy,

P. J. Barsby

the time honoured place
where girl meets a boy.
Gaily painted horses
of the roundabouts;
tall helter skelter,
gay laughter and shouts.
Clusters of bright lights
casting garish glow
on fun-seeking crowds
surging to and fro.

For three days there's joy
in this tented town.
Then the lights go out
and the stalls come down.

GOSSIP

Why is it that a friendly chat
can often turn to spite.
Malicious gossip meant to show
a neighbour in bad light.

What good can come of such a course?
What pleasure can be had
in spreading tales about a life
that may not be so bad.

We should remember when we chat
that far from being smart,
unfriendly gossip will degrade
the persons taking part.

GROWING UP

At one year old he cuts his teeth and starts a wobbly walk.
At two he rides a tricycle, and soon learns how to talk.

At five he is superior to little girls aged four.
At eight he doesn't play with them, at ten he's not so sure.

At twelve he thinks he knows it all, with patronising air.
At thirteen he is insecure, and starts to comb his hair.

At fourteen when among the girls, he's somewhat ill at ease
And blushes like a beetroot when they all set out to tease.

At sweet sixteen, and spotty faced, he starts to fall in love
And writes a lot of poetry about the stars above.

At eighteen he is much less gauche, and sports a jaunty air.
At twenty-one he's married to a girl with flaxen hair.

At twenty five, with family, he has to settle down,
With payments on the mortgage and a rather worried frown.

At thirty he becomes aware that he is getting old
And looks back with nostalgia to days when he was bold.

At forty now, with thinning hair and slightly bulging paunch
He takes up strenuous exercise, his thickening girth to staunch.

At sixty he looks forward to the age of sixty five
When he can give up going to work, and old hobbies revive.

At seventy he congratulates himself on reaching such a stage,
And all his friends agree with him he doesn't look his age.

At eighty he is laid to rest, well in the sere and yellow,
With tributes at the funeral, "A well respected fellow!"

P. J. Barsby

GYPSIES

Picturesque vans, gleaming brass.
Horses tethered, cropping grass.

Smell of woodsmoke in the air
Bits of harness here and there.

Washing pegged among the trees
drying in the evening breeze

Ear-ringed old men, kerchiefed hags,
Happy children, dressed in rags.

Clucking bantams, roaming dogs.
Pot a-boiling on small logs.

Supper ready, served from pot.
Stew and onions, piping hot.

Mellow sunlight fades away.
Dusk descending, end of day.

Swarthy faces, firelight glow
Swapping stories, voices low.

Pipes are lighted, tales are told
To the young ones by the old.

Of adventures long ago;
Of hard winters and deep snow.

Then the children go to bed,
As the sun sets fiery red.

Dogs are chained up, vans made fast.

Peace descends on camp at last.
These are gypsies, born to roam.
A caravan their humble home.

Yet a wondrous sight to see,
A camp of gypsies, wild and free.

HARASSED DAY *2

Hurry downstairs, slip on mat.
Falling sideways, sit on cat.
Milk boils over, burn the toast
Begging letters come through post

Arrived at office latest yet.
Boss is early, in a pet.
Then the call comes, "Bring your book!"
Take down letters, then I'm stuck.
Can't read outline, makes me mad
Shorthand getting very bad.

Junior brings in cup of tea,
Trips on chair leg, lands on me.
Dress and tights soaked, tea quite hot.
Jump up quickly, like I'm shot.

Chief clerk comes in, sees wet dress.
What's he thinking? You can guess.
"Now I know", says the young fool
"Why it's called the Typing Pool!".
Stands there grinning, like a chump.
I'd like to give him a jolly good thump.

---

2 Editor's note: This poem is very similar to "Just One Of Those Days". It is unclear which was intended to be the final version.

Why do I have days like these
when the fates seem hard to please.
Never mind, I'll learn to smile
And kid myself that life's worth while.

HARVEST FESTIVAL

The church is looking beautiful
with flowers down the aisles.
The congregation take their seats
exchanging nods and smiles.
There's fruit on all the windowsills,
and vegetables, too;
And happiness flows all around
from every well filled pew.

The service starts, the opening hymn
"We plough the fields and scatter"
bursts forth from every joyful heart
in praise of things that matter.
The choir process down the aisle,
and they with one accord
give of their best like all the rest
in praises to the Lord.

The autumn sunshine dapples through
the stained glass windows bright,
and lingers on the harvest gifts
which make a cheerful sight.
Of all the services in church
there's none that is so dear
as Harvest and its festival
the highlight of the year.

HOLIDAY FOR THE OVER 60s[3]

Grey heads, carefully coiffeured,
blue rinsed,
wispy white,
gather in the dining hall.
Cheerful chatter
concealing loneliness
and shyness.
Widows, spinsters in trouser suits
and flowered frocks
forget for a while
their rheumatism.
Bright evenings.
Eyes down for bingo.
Knees up Mother Brown.
Talent night.
Solo singing
in quavering tones,
savouring the applause
and unaccustomed limelight.
Coach tours,
and packed lunches.
Trips out,
and cosy cafes.
They'll take back memories
of a wonderful holiday,
when for a week
youth seemed to return,
and the cares of old age were forgotten.

---

[3] Editor's note: This poem is very similar to "Saga Holiday". It is unclear which was intended to be the final version.

P. J. Barsby

HOLIDAY SNAP *

We had been for a swim
and dried in the sun
lying on towels
after a run.
Then this photo you took
of me lying there
and I one of you
so we could share.
We rested awhile
before leaving the sands,
walked back to our lodgings
holding hands.

Parted on Saturday,
left the South Shore.
You vowing you'd love me
'for evermore'.
Said our goodbyes
on Central Station,
journeying home
in meditation.

It's twenty years since
your first letter came
with this photograph
in its plastic frame.
As I look at the snapshot
recalling the scene,
I can't help but ponder
on what might have been.

HOME *

Day after day, the blazing sun
    glares down on hard-baked earth.
The air is still, and nothing moves
    of life there is a dearth
There is no respite from the heat,
    until the humid night,
made eerie by the flitting moths
    attracted by the light
of lamp outside mosquito net,
    so I can see the better
to read the welcome news from home
    sent in an air-mailed letter.
And as I read, my mind goes back
    to days of yesteryear.
Of England's green and pleasant land
    and all that I hold dear.

Ah, give me just one day of rain,
    a day of clouds and mist.
A day when hedgerow and the fields
    with dewdrops have been kissed.
Then let me from my cottage home
    see once again the dawn,
and hear the cheerful song of birds
    on cool and Spring-like morn.
Let me just smell the rain-drenched dust
    of winding country lane,
and breathe once more the wine-like air
    that follows summer rain.
My grey-sky'd homeland, cool and lush
    there's nothing to compare
with a Spring-like day in England.
    Oh, would that I were there.

P. J. Barsby

HOUSING DEVELOPMENT

I watched the bulldozer
scarifying the landscape
like a devil monster
with a grudge against
the countryside.

Hedges were being grubbed up,
slender saplings uprooted
and churned to shreds
to satisfy the gaping maw
of this soul-less juggernaut.

Soon the pleasant field
was a muddy mess,
and the birds stopped singing.
Except for the agonised cries
of a pair of blackbirds,
bewailing the destruction
of their home and family.

IN PRAISE OF A GARDEN *

This enchanting, quiet garden,
Solace for the troubled spirit.
Resting place for the weary soul.
What happy, precious hours are spent
in your secluded, charming depths
in quiet contemplation
as the busy world goes by.

That patch of garden near the wall
where wax-like snowdrops in a ring
gave promise of an early Spring,
is now ablaze with daffodils,
and on the wall a blackbird trills.

34

The subtle fragrance of the rose
gives pleasure to inhaling nose.
Its thorny stem protects its charm
from vandal hand and reaching arm.

Sweet honeysuckle on the wall
twines lazily and grows quite tall.
Cool dark green hedge where dunnocks nest
and Robin flaunts his blood red chest.

Trim lawn where thrush and blackbird vie
to feast on bread-crumbs, wary eye
on figure seated in a chair,
relaxing in the scented air.

Each season brings its own content
with quiet time in garden spent.
Perhaps the Summer is the best
with sunshine, flowers, peaceful rest.

IN PRAISE OF BLUE

Blue is the colour of happy skies
The colour of a new-born baby's eyes.
The colour of distances and space.
The colour that has a soothing grace.
The colour of a bluetit on the hedge
and a kingfisher at the water's edge.
The colour of bluebells in a wood
on a summer evening, when life is good.
Blue of all colours is the most kind.
A colour that soothes and refreshes the mind.

P. J. Barsby

JEALOUSY (1) [4]

When she agreed to go out with him
he was over the moon.
She was so beautiful,
he couldn't believe
she cared for him, more than others.
After that first date,
his love blossomed, along with
a seed of jealousy.

He took to waiting for her
outside her place of work;
jealous of her male colleagues
in the office; jealous when she spoke
of the good time
at the office party;
jealous when she praised
another for his humour.

He wanted assurance of her love,
solely for himself,
not shared with others.
She told him not to be so possessive,
that his jealousy
was killing her love.
He still sees her
with her husband and family,
his love affair long gone
and the jealousy that killed it.

36

JEALOUSY (2)

When she agreed to go out with him,
he was ecstatic
She was so beautiful,
he couldn't believe
she cared for him, more than others.
After that first date,
his love blossomed, along with
a seed of jealousy.

He took to waiting for her
outside her place of work;
jealous of her male colleagues
in the office when she spoke
of the good time she had
at the office party;
jealous when she laughed at
another's humour
more than his own.

He wanted assurance of her love
solely for himself,
not shared with others.
She told him
not to be so possessive;
that his jealousy
was killing her love.

He still sees her occasionally
with her husband and family,
his love affair long past,
and the jealousy that killed it,
but can't help pondering
what might have been.

P. J. Barsby

JOURNEY'S END

The screaming jet
eats up the years
of separation,
winging like a bird
to the new world.

Excitement mounts, as
we circle the busy airport
rushing up to greet us.
Somewhere among those
ant-like figures on the ground
you are waiting
The jet whines to a stop,
taxies to the terminal.

I scan the blur of faces,
feeling alone, apprehensive.
Then I see you
standing there, waving.

A crescendo of heartbeats
mingle at mutual recognition.
The long wait is over,
and only you and I can know
the sweetness of the moment,
trembling on the air as
our arms enfold,
crushing the pent-up feelings
of aeons of time.
Our lips meet,
and the world stands still.

JUST ONE OF THOSE DAYS[5]

Hurry downstairs, slip on mat.
Falling sideways, sit on cat.

Milk boils over, burn the toast
Rates and gas bills come through post

Dash to station, sudden rain.
No umbrella, miss the train

Reach the office, late and wet.
Boss is early, in a pet.

Phone is ringing, boss wants file.
It's been missing quite a while.

Soon the call comes, "bring your book!"
Take down letters, then I'm stuck.

Can't read outline, makes me mad
Shorthand getting very bad.

Junior brings in cup of tea,
Trips on chair leg, lands on me.

Dress and tights soaked, tea quite hot.
Jump up quickly, like I'm shot.

Chief clerk comes in, sees wet dress.
What's he thinking? You can guess.

---

[5] Editor's note: This poem is very similar to "Harassed Day". It is unclear which was intended to be the final version.

P. J. Barsby

"Now I know", says the young fool
"Why it's called the typing pool!".

Stands there grinning, like a chump.
I'd like to give him a jolly good thump.

Why do I have days like these
when the fates seem hard to please.

Never mind, I'll learn to smile
And kid myself that life's worth while.

LAMENT *

Today, this country once so great
is passing through a cloud.
There's disobedience of the law
and mob rule by the crowd.

The attitude of many folk
to something they dislike,
is down their tools and break the rules
and promptly go on strike.

The harm they do is brushed aside -
who cares about the loss
of goodwill, exports, and prestige -
we'll show 'em who is boss!

The papers and the radio
and television too,
record the baser side of man,
the antics of the few.

The great majority of folk

are decent, peaceful souls
who live in some obscurity
and seldom reach their goals.

But when our Country's really down
or threatened by some appear,
justifying the tribesman's faith
in the miracle of Nature.

LIVING IN THE TWENTIETH CENTURY

The young man's motorbike next door
starts off the day with frightening roar.
A shattering pneumatic drill
outside my window makes me ill.
So in despair I go out shopping
and hope the rain will soon be stopping.

Head bent under dripping brolly,
to cross the road is utter folly,
with cars and buses speeding by
sending wet spray almost waist high.
Scuttling across, no time for pride,
eventually reach the other side.

Go in the store, let down my brolly,
Get bumped in back by passing trolley.
Eventually complete my shopping,
Still no sign of the deluge stopping.
Emerge from store with bags piled high
as home-bound bus goes speeding by.

With aching arms arrive back home
to find a load of soil has come.
They've dumped it just inside the gate,
the path and flowerbeds in a state.

The gas men come to find a leak,
they say they'll be here all next week.
The telephone is ringing loud.
I'm shattered, but my head's unbowed.
Living in the twentieth century?
It's quieter in the penitentiary!

MARCH

Shattering rain
on the window pane,
and a howling gale
like a banshee's wail.
Then a Spring-like day,
and the flowers bloom;
and winter's gloom
is cast away.

There's a touch of madness
in the air.
Birds are mating
everywhere.
The wily old hare,
as mad as a hatter,
flicks tail in the air
while all the rooks chatter.

This coming of Spring
is a wonderful thing;
when life stirs anew,
and we humans renew
our faith in Creation,
as the wakening land
shows us such beauty
on every hand.

So welcome, March!
Your boisterous weather
sweeps Winter away,
bringing together
the lengthening days
and sunlit hours;
rebirth from the dead,
and Springtime flowers.

NOTE TO OUR NOISY NEIGHBOURS

We are your neighbours, not really unkind
And your climbing children we don't mind.
Even their shouting in the garden
doesn't make our arteries harden.
But when you have your weekend party,
need your guests be quite so hearty
when they depart, with slamming car doors,
and revving their engines without pause?
While on other nights your screaming child
and constant hammering makes us wild.
Surely we have quite enough to contend
with your blaring hi-fi for hours on end.
We don't wish to cause a quarrel, as such.
and hope that it's not really asking too much;
but we'd be grateful to you if the noise could cease
and we be allowed to live in peace.

NOTTINGHAM GOOSE FAIR

Faint snatches of music
colour the evening breeze.
A myriad bright lights
stab the darkness, scintillating
among the trees.

P. J. Barsby

All roads lead to the fair,
the helter-skelter the landmark.

Chivvied along by
good-humoured crowds,
the forest is reached.
The lights are dazzling,
the music raucus.

We enter the arena.
Pug nosed fighters
draped in dressing gowns
stand on lofted platform,
challenging all comers.
Scantily clad girls gyrate
in front of gaudy booth
full of Eastern promise.

We pass the barbaric Hall of Freaks,
the Wild West Show, the hot dog stall,
while candy-flossed crowds saunter aimlessly,,
content to be part of the scene, with
kiss-me-quick hats and tickling sticks.

Others seek thrills on the dodgems,
the cakewalk, the chairoplanes;
or try their skill with airgun and dart,.
while sticky-fingered children
with toffee apples.
cling to their mothers' skirts.

The clack of coconut shies
mingle with the cries of vendors
and the raucus music of the roundabouts.
For three days there's joy in this tented town
Then the lights go out, and the stalls come down.

ON ACCEPTING A RETIREMENT GIFT OF A TAPE-RECORDER

Thank you for this splendid gift, which I accept with pleasure.
It's something I have always wished and something I shall treasure.
I understand this gift to me was made with full accord,
and that the speeches have been taped to give me a record.
This is indeed a happy thought, and in the years ahead
I'll play this tape record again, and recall what was said..

For forty years I've served the firm in times both good and bad.
And now, on my retirement, I can't help feeling sad.
I've made so many worthy friends the time that I've been here,
and valued all your friendships more as year succeeded year.
And now I have to say farewell, but in my heart I know
The memory of your friendship here will keep my heart aglow.

OUR HERITAGE

Narrow country lanes
meandering from village to village
in timeless tranquillity.

Ancient coaching inns,
where ghosts of highwaymen
haunt cool taprooms.

Quiet backwaters, where
poling punt and sculling skiff
scarce ripple still waters.

Colour and pomp of ancient ceremonies,
unashamedly changeless
in a changing world.

P. J. Barsby

The game of cricket
played on village green
in relaxed atmosphere

where time stands still
for cups of tea and cucumber sandwiches
in white-painted pavilion.

Old churches, stately homes,
battle sites, and the interred bones
of long departed ancestors.

Circles, stones, monuments
and ancient tracks. .
Our heritage - let none relax!

OUT OF DARKNESS INTO LIGHT

The first experience, a baby is born
And nature responds each day with the dawn.
A miner coming up after working all night
appreciates the transition from darkness to light.
A man who was blind, for many years nothing has seen,
recovers his sight, and is amazed at the green
of the grass and the trees and the colour of flowers;
and discovers life's many exciting hours.
To a lesser degree, a steam train in a tunnel
emerges with joy, belching smoke from its funnel.
A problem that has been insoluble at night
seems less of a problem when faced in daylight.
The eskimo in his igloo, after months in the dark
sees the first rays of sun and is up like a lark.
These are the few of the things that delight,
Out of the darkness into the light

REQUIEM

I shed a tear
as the gun-carriage drew near
draped with the Union Jack.
My mind went back

to the day you came home on leave,
proud in your new uniform
which still retained its nap.
The badge on your cap

shone like burnished gold.
You were not very old -
too young to give your life
for a country torn with strife.

Yet your life has gone,
and as the carriage rumbles on
my heart rebels at the price
of your sacrifice.

SAGA HOLIDAY[6]

Grey heads
carefully coiffeured,
blue rinsed,
wispy white,
gather in the dining hall

Cheerful chatter
concealing loneliness

---

[6] Editor's note: This poem is very similar to "Holiday for the Over 60s". It is unclear which was intended to be the final version.

P. J. Barsby

and shyness.

Widows, spinsters, in trouser suit
and flowered frocks
forget for awhile
their rheumatism.

Bright evenings,
Eyes down for bingo,
Knees Up Mother Brown.
Solo singing
in quavering tones,
savouring the applause
and unaccustomed limelight

Coach tours
and packed lunches.
Trips out
and cosy cafes.
They'll take back memories
of a wonderful holiday,
when for awhile
youth seemed to return
and old age infirmities
were forgotten.

SCHOOL DAYS

I remember the school where I went as a boy
And the various games I used to enjoy.
The insistent 'ding, ding' of the little school bell
As we hurried to school as though drawn by a spell.

I remember the noise and the shouting at play
And the smell of the playground on a wet day.

I remember being sent from the room in disgrace
And returning much later with bright crimson face.

There was football at playtime, hard knocks with a smile
And collecting cigarette cards which lasted a while.
There was singing on Fridays in late afternoon
The girls singing sweetly, the boys out of tune.

We had lessons, of course, which were sometimes a bore.
And a kindly headmaster, who taught us much more
than the way to do sums and to write and to spell.
He taught us the value of doing things well.

And though in old age many things I forget
Respect for that headmaster stays with me yet.

SHERWOOD FOREST

We stand before the Major Oak,
  a venerable tree
A thousand years of history seen,
  and many more will see.
Set in this noble forest, in
  the famous Sherwood glades
Where Robin and his Merrie Men
  lay hidden in the shades.
This grand old tree, its branches gnarled
  and needing now support,
Was once the trysting place of brave men
  outlawed by the Court.
And close by was another tree
  that stood from year to year,
Where Robin hung the venison
  from many a noble deer.
In nearby church at Edwinstowe
  the legends firmly state

The outlaw married Marian
  his life-long faithful mate.

Hark! what was that? I thought I heard
  the faint sound of a horn
Among the rustle of the leaves
  by forest breezes borne.
Crouch on the ground, don't make a sound
  and we shall surely see
The outlaws in their Lincoln green
  still roving, proud and free.

STARTING SCHOOL *

A hot little hand clutched firmly in mine.
Little steps taking him to a new world.
Memories of childhood come flooding my mind.
Frightening, exciting, that first day at school.

What is he saying, "Has the teacher a cane?"
"Of course not, my darling!" I squeeze his hand tight.
"There are lots of nice toys, a rocking horse, too
And plenty of children to play with, like you".

We reach the school gates. "Mummy, why can't you stay?"
"Mummies don't go to school" - what else could I say.
"I'll be waiting outside when you come out at twelve".
He puts on a brave face and tries hard to smile.

I turn my head quickly, my eyes prick with tears.
A smiling young teacher takes hold of his hand
At the gates I turn round, but they have now gone
Into the corridor of his new world.

Blindly, unseeing, I walk home alone.
Still feeling the clutch of his hot little hand.

STORM AT SEA

Thunder rolls incessantly, the rain comes sheeting down.
Forked lightning lights up vividly the nearby coastal town.
The towering waves lash shingled beach, and hiss as they recede.
Borne on the breeze, faint cries for help from one in dire need.

Alarm is sounded, lifeboat launched with haste in seconds few.
The engine roars, on board the boat sit tense the gallant crew.
Careening like a Viking prow, the boat rides cresting wave.
The grim-faced crew are silent now, their thoughts a life to save.

At last they reach the upturned boat, the man cries out "I'm here!"
A life-jacket attached to line is thrown, but in his fear
His frozen fingers fail to grasp the help. In agony
They see the man slip from the boat and vanish in the sea.

Without a pause the coxon dives into the surging sea,
Supported by a crew-held line while floating helplessly
The man is tossed from wave to wave but ever drawing near
To where the sturdy coxon swims, without a sign of fear.

The man is reached and brought aboard, resuscitation given.
At last his breathing starts again, the coxon says "Thank Heaven".
The crew return in triumph to their station on the shore.
Another task completed but - there will be many more.

STRANGE DREAM *

I have this strange recurring dream
that I'm flying round a room. I seem
with arms outstretched to fly at will
and feel exalted by my skill.

But then it seems that all at once
I lose my skill, and feel a dunce

P. J. Barsby

as on the bed with quite a thump
I land as if I've made a jump.

Can anyone tell me what this means,
and whether others have such dreams?

TEENAGER [*]

"Can anyone , hate you, hate you.
My voice rose to a shriek
I stamped my foot in anger
and tears ran down my cheek.

"Why must I be in at midnight
when the dance goes on till two?"
My father replied calmly
"It's much too late for you.

With muggers on the streets at night
and sometimes rapists, too.
I don't want you to be alone
when coming home at two".

"My boyfriend says he'll bring me home,
and will look after me.
I promise you we'll come straight home
and be on time, you'll see".

That night my father had a stroke.
A week and he was dead.
And now those words are haunting me,
I didn't mean, but said.

TERMINUS

Arrive at the terminus
Day's journey done.
Collect our belongings
Set off for home.

Arrive at the terminus
Life's journey run.
But for the believer
It's "welcome home".

THE AWAKENING

The days have been dreary,
the nights have been cold
The trees have been bare
and looking so old.
The ground has been covered
quite deeply in snow
and it seems most unlikely
the flowers will grow.

But then comes the sunshine,
we bask in its rays,
and notice with pleasure
the lengthening days.
Come snowdrops and crocus,
and all the birds sing;
and we realise with wonder
It's once again Spring.

P. J. Barsby

THE BROOCH *

A diamond brooch in a second-hand shop
Caught my eyes as I passed and caused me to stop.
A perfect example of jeweller's art,
It had a strange beauty that tugged at my heart.
The filligree work was exceedingly fine,
and I felt I would never rest till it was mine.

So I went in and bought it, the price was quite high;
But I just couldn't let such a bargain go by.
As the shopkeeper wrapped it in tissue with care
I knew that I had a possession most rare.

I muse on its history and wonder what year
It was perhaps bought for a person most dear.
A friend who had treasured it, loved it as well
Then did some adversity force her to sell?

I gaze on its beauty and know in my heart
I shall keep it for always, and never shall part
With this token of love which gave so much pleasure
To its previous owner, and now mine to treasure.

THE BRIDE

Modestly veiled, and gowned in lace
An ethereal beauty of form and face
A vision of loveliness and grace
She stands beside her groom.

And never did a lovelier bride
stand by a handsome bridegroom's side.
She looks at him with love and pride
this special afternoon.

What thoughts are in that pretty head
as now the marriage vows are said?
She's looking radiant, though it's said
she cried in her own room.

But as they come back down the aisle,
gone are the fears she had awhile.
There's on her face a loving smile
Shared with her handsome groom.

THE CAT

Grace and beauty as she lies there
Sprawled across the lamb's wool rug.
Stretching in luxurious comfort
Gently licking bended paw.

Enigmatic, half-closed eyelids
Gaze as though with thoughts afar
As she stops her endless preening
To watch mistress in the chair.

Then without a second's warning,
Silent bound and she is up.
Beating soft tattoo with front paws,
Seeking comfort in the lap.

Purring like a well-tuned engine
In a chassis sleek and trim.
Dreaming of the Heaven cats dream of
Sure, that purring is a hymn!

P. J. Barsby

THE CHURCH ON THE HILL

The pointing spire rises clear
of the council housing estate
desecrating the landscape below.
Once, there were fields
starred with buttercups and daisies,
a languid stream meandering
round the wooded knoll,
where lovers idled
on a summer's evening.

The fields, the trees
have gone.
Lovers now stroll
in well-lit streets.
The sound of discos has replaced
the song of birds.
Cinemas blaze
their X-rated films.
Bingo halls are crowded,
the church half empty, but still
the spire rises proudly,
dominating the scene,
pointing to the sky
and castle in the air.

THE CROSS

He bore His Cross
in pain, humiliation,
yet with dignity
to save humanity.

Two thousand years
have gone. And now

a cross means no more
than a mark
on a voting paper,
or the signature
of an illiterate person.

Today, the cross
may mean yes,
or no
or don't know,
or draw attention to
a printing error.

To our loss
we seldom think
of the significance
of that other Cross.

THE DANCE

Twisting and twirling
in exotic gyrations
of wild abandon,
soundless as a lover's caress.
These are the dead,
dressed in their Autumn finery,
exulting in their freedom
before the remorseless Keeper
sweeps them into eternity.
Next year, others yet unformed
will take their places,
dancing to the gentle
sighing of the breeze
in Nature's autumn ballet -
the Dance of the Fallen leaves.

P. J. Barsby

THE DEADLINE

"Remember the deadline" urged the chief to his staff
repeated advice which became quite a laugh.
Then a reporter was sent to a ship in the dock
"And return with your story before three o'clock!"

The Captain was friendly, and soon called him chum
and supplied the reporter with large tots of rum.
They were both having such a convivial time.
The reporter forgot all about the deadline.

The Captain eventually finished his story
And how it had brought him both fame and some glory.
But sad to relate, when the reporter got back
His muddled up story only got him the sack.

THE FALLS

Entranced, I stood beside
the mighty falls. The roar
of foam-flecked water,
descending at awesome speed,
was frightening.
To speak, even to shout
was futile. The incessant roar
of nature at her wildest
dominated the scene. The spray
tattoed my cheeks, bringing a sense
of exhilaration.

And yet,

at home that evening,
in the quietness of the garden,
the song of a blackbird,

like a hymn of praise,
brought nearer the presence
of the Creator.

THE FAVOURITE

To some it may seem humble.
to others even low.
It has no choice description,
and does not make a show.
But when the stomach rumbles
with an empty, griping pain,
its aroma is like nectar
to the senses and the brain.

It isn't rich in colour.
It does not make a show.
But its delicious flavour
makes the gastric juices flow.

It has a fine aroma,
and it has its jeers and quips.
Yet there's nothing quite so tasty
as a wrapped up parcel of chips.

THE FRIEND

One who's there to intercede
One who helps you in your need.
One who has a soothing power
Calming you in darkest hour.
One who shares your grief and pain
And though rebuffed, comes back again.
One who knows your every mood
Does not condemn, does not intrude.

One who shares your happiness
As well as sorrow and distress.
One who's with you to the end.
Won't you let Him be your friend?

THE GUY

A little boy, so thin and wan
  stood on a busy street.
His clothes were ill-fitting and torn,
  with split shoes on his feet.
His cap lay on the pavement
  by a monstrous looking guy.
And every time a stranger passed
  he made the same old cry.
"A penny for the guy", he asked.
  and "Thank you very much"
He smiled a beatific smile
  each time he made a 'touch'.

And then a Bobby came along,
  and did I see him wink?
"You'll have to pack it up, me lad
  or else you'll be in clink".
"You can't go begging on the streets,
  'cos its agen the law,
And if I catch you here agen,
  I'll run you in for sure".

The lad picked up the monstrous guy
  and looked so full of woe.
I'm sure the Bobby blinked a bit
  as we both watched him go.
And then the policeman called him back,
  and with a sort of sigh,
Produced a coin, I heard him say
  "Here's something for the guy".

THE HANDSHAKE

It was done so very nicely, in such a kindly way.
"Sorry we're losing you, but..... a cheque for two years' pay.
"Been with the firm for thirty years? All that time ago?
We'll miss you, won't we, all you chaps? - it must be quite a blow.

I glanced around the office walls that I had known so well.
The zig-zag patterned wallpaper, and the familiar smell
that came from bales of calico stored in the large stock rooms
adjacent to the factory which housed the spinning looms.

And I mused on the years that I'd spent with the firm,
first as a junior clerk, then for a term
of ten years as a finance head, consulted by the board.
And now I'm made redundant by that very self-same board.

I've saved the old firm thousands in taxes and the like.
I've worked late in the evenings and never been on strike.
So now that I'm redundant, I would ask them to refute
That it's not a golden handshake, but a two-fingered salute!

THE HEDGEHOG

At dusk you'll see him cross the lane,
avoiding any cars that pass,
until he gains the other side
and pauses on the bordered grass.
Then in a garden makes his way,
where he will stay until the dawn;
and eagerly await the dish
of food set out upon the lawn.

Inoffensive, slow and pensive,
the hedgehog is the gardener's friend;
eating insects, slugs, and beetles -

of his goodness there is no end.
So if you see the humble creature
in your garden at end of day.
Put out dish of milk and breadcrumbs
and encourage him to stay.

THE LAST TRIP

In better days she had been
pampered like a pet.
Trim chassis kept sleek, shining.
waxed polished, immaculate.
Until that last fatal trip,
never completed.

Now she sits astride a junk heap
in the breaker's yard;
blank gaze from
sightless lamp sockets
staring fixedly
into bleak unknown,
waiting in vain
for her owner's return.

Was that the wind
closing swinging door,
or was it his spirit
once again taking the wheel
of his beloved Cortina,
now perched,
rusting and forlorn,
on top of the heap.
The body sways gently
in the evening breeze.
Rays from the setting sun

give gleam to sightless sockets,
and for fleeting seconds
the chromium grill
seems to wear
a sunlit smile.

THE OLD ACTOR

The lure of the footlights was strong in his blood
Many parts he had played, his acting was good.
Fans in their thousands did his genius acclaim,
And for many long years he enjoyed world-wide fame.

But the public is fickle. As time went by
His engagements diminished, don't ask me why.
Until the day came when he hadn't a part,
And the public forgot his consummate art.

Many years later, a man of great age
Could be found helping out with the props backstage.
Then one night they found him, they all heard him fall.
The actor had taken his last curtain call.

A brief note in the Press recalled his past fame
And once more the public remembered his name.
The theatre had been in his blood, they said.
But none were aware how his heart had bled.

THE PUNJAB

Plodding bullock pulls
primitive plough
guided by turbanned gaunt figure
in dhoti and pantaloons.
Brassy sun glares down

on arid plain.
No birds sing. The silence
can be felt. The plough
hitting a stone,
sounds like a rifle shot
in the still air.
The seed is set in faith,
waiting for the monsoon.
Then,
little green shoots will appear,
justifying the tribesman's faith
in the miracle of Nature.

THE RESCUE

Thunder rolls incessantly, the rain comes sheeting down.
Forked lightning lights up vividly the nearby coastal town.
The towering waves lash pebbled beach, and hiss as they recede.
Borne on the breeze come cries for help from one in dire need.

Alarm is sounded, lifeboat launched with haste in seconds few.
The engine roars, on board the boat sit tense the gallant crew.
Careening like a Viking prow, the boat rides cresting wave.
The grim-faced crew are silent now, their thoughts a life to save.

At last they reach the upturned boat, the man cries out "I'm here!"
A life-jacket attached to line is thrown, but in his fear
His frozen fingers fail to grasp the help. In agony
They see the man slip from the boat and vanish in the sea.

Without a pause the coxon dives into the surging foam.
Supported by a crew held line to bring him safely home.
The man is tossed from wave to wave but ever drawing near
To where the sturdy coxon swims, without a sign of fear.

At last the man is brought aboard, resuscitation given.
And when his breathing starts again, the coxon says "Thank Heaven".
The crew return in triumph to their station on the shore.
Another task completed, but - there will be many more.

THE THRUSH

He sits on a bough as
  the day draws to its close;
trilling a melody
  as though he would compose
a song of thanksgiving
  to his Maker on high,
for his food and his safety,
  his freedom to fly

One minute he sits there -
  the next he has gone.
Leaving me uplifted
  by his beautiful song.

THE VOICE ON THE TELEPHONE

Deep and resonant
timbred with pleasant tones
like an organ softly played,
the voice of the countryman
comes through the telephone.

I see a man of middle age
lean and wiry, grey grizzled hair;
weather-browned face, skin wrinkled
like a ripened russet apple.
Rough tweeds, redolent with

P. J. Barsby

the scent of ripening hay.
The unhurried movements
of a man of the soil.

The voice ceases, the receiver
is replaced. And for fleeting seconds
a breath of the countryside
seems to linger round the
now silent telephone.

THOSE DANCING YEARS (1)[7]

A ribboned card of dances
dated Nineteen Twenty Eight.
What happy memories it invokes,
what memories to relate.

I hear again the beat of jazz
played at its very best.
The Charleston and the Black Bottom,
The One-Step and the rest.

I see once more bobbed hair and bandeau
and sequined shimmering frocks
above the knees of silk clad legs,
and girls in sleeveless smocks;
the men in Oxford Bags and blazers
sitting all around
while saxophone and violin
excited with their sound.

---

[7] Editor's note: There are two versions of "Those Dancing Years". It is unclear
which was intended to be the final version. Both are included.

66

And I recall the melodies
that made those days unique;
'When You and I Were Seventeen'
as we danced cheek to cheek.

'My Souvenirs' and 'Tea for Two'
'The Blue Room' and 'Girl Friend'
and 'Bye Bye, Blackbird'- ah, we thought
those days would never end.

And now, alas, those days are gone,
old age has come at last.
But it brings pleasure to recall
these memories of the past.

THOSE DANCING YEARS (2)

A ribboned card of dances
dated Nineteen-Twenty-five.
What happy memories it invokes,
what happy hours revive.
I hear again the beat of jazz
played at its very best;
the Charleston and the Black Bottom,
the One-Step and the rest.

I see once more bobbed hair and bandeau;
sequined shimmering frocks
above the knees, and silk-clad legs,
and girls in sleeveless smocks;
with men in Oxford Bags and blazers
sitting all around
while saxophone and violin
excited with their sound.

And I recall the melodies
that made those days unique;
'When You and I were Seventeen'
as we danced cheek to cheek.
'My Souvenirs', and 'Tea for Two';
'The Blue Room' and 'Girl Friend'
and 'Bye Bye, Blackbird'- ah, we thought
those days would never end.

And now, alas, those days are gone,
old age has come at last;
but it brings pleasure to recall
these memories of the past.

WINTER

There's something sad
about trees in winter.
standing silent, with bare branches
etched against a lowering sky;
as though waiting, uncomplaining,
for the return of Spring.

In the glare of our headlights
they take on the appearance
of ghostly figures, gliding towards us,
with branches outstretched,
as though to implore us,
"Leave us undisturbed
in our long winter sleep!"

Haiku

Haiku is a form of traditional Japanese poetry having meters of 5-7-5 syllables.

A slow moving stream
gives a sense of timelessness
and tranquility

Softly played music
can create nostalgic joy
or melancholy.

A book and a pipe
is a solace and pleasure
to a lonely man.

Intense jealousy
may kill the tender blossom
of mutual love.

Byron - a legend
that gives his priceless poems
immortality.

Byron - a legend
good poems, bad behaviour
immortality.

pussy asleep

P. J. Barsby

on my chair
snooze on settee

In the post office
queue getting longer
tempers shorter

A single gunshot
on a calm summer's evening
spells death on the nature reserve

A slow moving stream
giving sense of timelessness
until a fish plops

My erstwhile lover
passes me by, ignoring me
an old scar twitches

Nottingham City
birthplace of General Booth
Statue - Robin Hood

Nottingham City
Home of General Booth
statue of Robin Hood

Nottingham birth-place
Salvation Army's founder
Robin Hood's statue.
Across the meadow

the sound of church bells calling
a faithful feels guilt

Bearers in black
bearing burden on shoulders
the mourners sorrow in hearts.

Jokes

"Was it crowded at the student's ball last night?"
"Not under our table!"

Hello, Billy. Is your sister expecting me?
Yes, said the little brat.
How do you know?
She's gone out.

So you think Dora's face is her fortune.
I'm sure of it. It runs into a nice little figure.

Professor: You say there is a collector at the door. Did you tell
him I was out?
Yes sir, but he didn't believe me.
Professor: Well, I'd better go and tell him myself.

Pretty caller: "Do you think the manager will see me now?"
Clerk: "Certainly, madam, the manager always has time to see
pretty girls"
Pretty caller: "Well, tell him that his wife is here".

"I want to buy a train set for my little boy".
"Yes sir, next floor, Men's Hobbies".

"What is your son going to be when he passes his final exams?"
"An old age pensioner".

"They tell me your son in college is quite an author"
"Does he write for money?"
"Yes, in every letter".
Teacher: "You shouldn't say 'I aint going'. You should say 'I am not going'. 'He is not going' 'They are not going' 'We are not going' "You are not going'."
The pupil's reply was 'Aint nobody going?'

"Why did you give the cloakroom attendant a dollar tip?"
"Where else can you get a fur coat for a dollar?"

DOTTY DEFINITIONS

Abundance	Playful rabbits
Aroma	One who cannot settle down.
Attire	Pertaining to a bicycle.
Blunderbuss	Omnibus which fails to stop
Capsize	Mark in hatband.
Carbide	Garage
Cargo	Petrol
Champaign	To pretend to be hurt
Dandelion	Fine specimen of the King of Beasts
Dragon	A lengthy sermon
Detergent	A policeman
Extradition	Late evening paper
Funicular	Sign of illness
Fustian	A tramp
Handicap	Useful headgear
Holy Office	The boss's sanctum

CRAZY CROSS-TALK
Between BOB and JACK

BOB: You're supposed to be clever. Which travels faster, heat or cold?

JACK: Heat, because you can catch a cold.

BOB: Clever dick. What's the difference between a lemon, an orange, and a banana?

JACK: Don't know.

BOB: Caught you this time. If you don't know, it's a good job your wife doesn't send you shopping on your own.

BOB: There's a rumour going round that Freddie Forbes has lost a lot of money. Would it be Preferred stock?

JACK: No, preferred blondes.

BOB: You're a betting man. What happens to the horses you follow?

JACK: Oh, they usually follow the other horses.

BOB: Talking about the beef problem, I've eaten beef all my life and I'm as strong as an ox.

JACK: That's funny. I've eaten fish all my life and I can't swim a stroke!

BOB: Who's that chap who has just gone by? He looks a bit down in the mouth.

JACK: We call him Adam. Whenever illnesses are mentioned, he's always 'ad 'em.

BOB: I wonder why people put candles on their birthday cakes.

JACK: Probably to make light of their age, I suppose.

JACK: Speaking of ages, I've got a good memory for my age. I can remember every name in three pages of a telephone directory.

BOB: Go on, try.

JACK: Right. Smith, Smith, Smith, Smith, Smith -------

BOB: Clever dick. Now tell me why they call our language the mother tongue.

JACK: I suppose it's because father seldom gets the chance to use it at home.

BOB: What makes you think John's an optimist?

JACK: What else can you call a man who does crosswords with a pen?

BOB: My wife says if I don't give up golf she will leave me.

JACK: I say, that's a bit hard, isn't it?

BOB: Yes, I shall miss her.

JACK: There goes old Jim. He's a pillow of our church.

BOB: Don't you mean a pillar of the church?

JACK: No, he sleeps during the sermons.

JACK: Did you like Joan's maternity ring?

BOB: Don't you mean 'eternity' ring?

JACK: No, it's one of those expanding rings.

BOB: As a friend of yours, perhaps I ought to tell you that Jim Johnson is going round telling all sorts of lies about you.

JACK: Oh, that's O.K. But if ever he starts telling the truth, I'll break his neck!

P. J. Barsby

YOUR PROBLEMS SOLVED

By Auntie Dotty.

My postbag this week has been particularly heavy.

Thank you, "Worried, Wimbledon" for pointing out the brick I dropped last week. Am sending you a length of thin cord which should make you a nice necklace.

Many of you seem to be having trouble with your boy friends, so I am devoting this week's page to typical queries I have received. It may help others who have the same problems.

"When my boy friend comes to see me, he often suggests we should go all the way. What should I do?"
It all depends which way he wants to go. If it is too far, tell him your feet are killing you.

"Although I am 18, I rarely have any dates. Can you help?"
I don't like the sticky things, either. Try prunes.

"My young man has been courting me for 17 years. Do you think he really loves me?"
Well, if he does, he has amazing staying power. He may be a late developer.

"I have fallen for the boy in the flat below".
Oh dear, I hope you didn't hurt yourself. Next time, use the lift.

"My boy friend has left me for another girl. What has she got that I haven't got?"
Nothing, dear, but perhaps hers are more attractive.

"My husband has such a high pitched voice he can break a wine glass with his singing".
Sounds as though he is a bit of a crackpot.

"My boy friend is always complaining that I am flat chested. Is there anything I can do about it?"
Sorry, but I'm afraid you will have to stick it out.

"I always have pimples when my young man kisses me. Why is this?"
You shouldn't be such a silly goose.

"My boy friend always closes his eyes when he kisses me. Why should he do this?"
I'm afraid only your mirror can tell you this, dear.

"I am a martyr to indigestion. Can you suggest anything?"
Always chew your food well, and as a martyr, make sure your halo is on straight.

"I get very stubborn at times and am not easily moved. Can you suggest how I can overcome this?"
This is a distressing complaint. Have you tried senna pods?

"My boy friend belongs to the Wandering Hand Society. What should I do?"
Don't worry, dear. It's a sign he has a certain feeling for you.

"My young man often suggests going to bed when he visits me in my flat. Why is this?"
Perhaps he's tired, poor dear. You could suggest very gently that

he has a nap before he comes.

"I am trying to trace my family tree. Can you tell me how to go about it?"
Yes, Mrs. Rose, I certainly can. Obtain a grower's catalogue, cut out a photograph of the appropriate tree, and trace it with a fine pen.

"My husband's face is very bristly and makes me sore when he kisses me. Can you suggest anything?"
Knit him a Balaclava helmet.

"I am marrying a man named Strife. Do you think I ought to change my first name, which is Lotta?"
Well, if you don't I can see there will be a Lotta Strife. Why not ask him to change his name to Pleasure? There would then be a Lotta Pleasure.

Well, that's all for this week, girls. Keep your letters rolling in!

Your friendly

AUNTIE DOTTY

Limericks

A pretty young Miss became Mrs.
And smothered her husband with krs
Her husband said "Titch
Though we may not be rich
We'll certainly know what True Brs".

There was a young lady named Banker
Who slept while the ship was at anchor.
She awoke in dismay
When she heard the mate say,
"Now haul up the topsheet, and spanker!"

The Sultan, annoyed with his harem,
Invented a scheme for to scare 'em.
He caught him a mouse
Which he loosed in the house
(The confusion is called harem scarem).

A cheerful old bear at the Zoo
Could always find something to do.
When it bored him, you know
To walk to and fro
He reversed it, and walked fro and to.

There once was a lonesome, lorn spinster
Whose luck for years had been ag'inster
When a man came to burgle
She shrieked, with a gurgle
"Stop,thief!, while I call in a Min'ster.

P. J. Barsby

There was an old man, who said "Hush!
I perceive a bird in this bush"
When they said, "Is it small?"
He replied, "Not at all,
It's nearly as big as the bush".

Short Stories

Percy wrote many short stories. The underlying themes are of love and surprise.

The stories are arranged in alphabetical order by title.

A BUMP IN THE NIGHT

Jack Higgins was obsessed with his home made radio set. Admittedly, it had taken him many hours to build, and quite a lot of money, too. But it was his hobby, something to keep him interested in life since he retired

He was working on a circuit of his own design, and his great ambition was to pick up an American station, but so far without success. Perhaps he should try a new tuning coil. His thoughts were interrupted by his wife's voice.

"For goodness sake stop fiddling with that wireless set and let's get off to bed!" Mrs. Higgins was getting a little peeved, having to remain quiet while her husband was tinkering with his wireless set.

"Oh, all right", sighed Jack. "Just another five minutes", and he cautiously continued to turn the tuning knob so as not to miss any foreign station.

"Well, I'm going to bed now". Mrs. Higgins put away her knitting. "And don't forget to switch the light off when you come up".

It was another ten minutes before Jack went to bed, and by that time his wife was asleep. As he undressed, his mind still grappled with the problem of getting America. He could pick up some of the Continental stations quite clearly, but when it came to the American wavebands his set didn't respond. He would try a new tuning coil tomorrow night when Elsie had gone to bingo. And with these thoughts in mind, he got into bed and was soon asleep.

It seemed to him only five minutes later when he wakened with a hazy recollection of hearing a sound downstairs. He was a light sleeper, and any unusual sound disturbed him. He sat up, now wide awake, and listened intently.

Somewhere in the distance a goods train rattled on its way, while nearer at hand a lorry rumbled along the main road. Just the ordinary sounds of the night. He began to feel relieved, although he still had the feeling that something unusual had wakened him. Of course it might have been the people next door, they kept such late hours and seemed to slam the car doors when they came in. He couldn't hear them now, though - he really must have been mistaken. And snoodling down again between the sheets, he began to doze off.

It was then that he heard it again, a faint sound like a chair being moved or bumped against. It came from downstairs. Again he sat up in bed, this time with a creepy sensation down his spine. There it was again - a kind of scratching sound. Someone was moving about downstairs!

At the thought of burglarism, Jack shivered. Suppose they were armed, he wouldn't stand much chance against two armed hulking brutes. Perhaps there was only one - perhaps it wasn't a burglar at all. It might be a policeman who had found a door unlocked or a window catch unfastened. But he felt sure that the doors were locked and the windows fastened.

He continued to listen, undecided what to do. He wasn't really a coward but somehow he felt terribly frightened now. He had never imagined burglars breaking into his house and the thought that they were downstairs at this very moment terrified him. He had a sudden wild inclination to bury his head under the bedclothes and forget all about it, or at least pretend he hadn't heard anything. Then he wouldn't have to face them, and could appear just as surprised as his wife in the morning when they found the house had been burgled. No, he couldn't allow them to get away with their valuables. He would stop them somehow.

A curious feeling ran through him as he made this decision. Perhaps it was the blood of his ancestors stirring at the thought of battle. Should he waken Elsie? No, perhaps he had better not, she might only scream and scare the intruders away with their valuables.

He got out of bed and stood for a moment while he decided what to use as a weapon. They lived in an old fashioned house with a fireplace in the bedroom, but long ago they had installed a gas fire so there wasn't even a poker. Then he remembered the heavy brass candlesticks on the dressing table, those antique candlesticks he had bought at a sale, and which Elsie had told him was a sheer waste of money. Yes, one of them would make a formidable weapon.

Shuffling into his slippers, he made his way to the dressing table and picked up one of the candlesticks. The feel of the old heavy brass gave him confidence. He reviewed his plan of attack. He would creep down- stairs, throw open the door of the living room, and before the surprised burglars had time to realise what was happening, he would crack them over the head, like that. And he suppressed a cry of pain as his arm connected with a corner of the tallboy.

Rubbing his arm, he slowly descended the stairs. The bottom tread creaked alarmingly. It sounded like the crack of a pistol to his excited fancy, and he remained still for a moment, mentally blasting the stair but hardly daring to breathe. As he listened, he caught the sound of subdued voices. His heart thumped violently. There was no doubt at all now, someone was in the living room.

Tightening his grip on the candlestick, he slowly crossed the hall at the foot of the stairs and made his way along the passage. From beneath the living room door, a faint gleam of light was visible.

And now the voices were quite distinct, though subdued. Again the creepy sensation trickled down his spine. Carefully feeling his way he approached the door. He had nearly got there when he caught his slipper on a sunken tile in the passage, and stumbled slightly. Instinctively he put his arm out to save himself, and scraped the candlestick on the wall. It was only a slight sound but the burglars must have heard him, as the voices ceased abruptly.

It was no use waiting now. The longer he waited the more prepared they would be. Swiftly he threw open the door, the candlestick raised ready to strike. He stopped, amazed. The room seemed exactly as he had left it, except that the light was on. He was sure he hadn't left the light on when he went to bed. Then, from a corner of the room, a voice spoke.

"Well folks, that's the end of our chat show. But stay with us for the old timers' Country and Western group". Then, after a pause, "You are tuned in to Radio Pittsburg. Sit back and get your feet tapping to the music".

Jack's mouth opened in astonishment. The voices had been coming from the radio. He sat down in sheer relief. And he had been sitting there fully a minute before he realised the programme was coming from America.

Chuckling with joy, he went over to his beloved set, noting the dial setting and the wavelength. Why hadn't he got this station before? Probably because of the time lag, he must have been tuning in before they came on the air.

In a happy frame of mind he switched off the set, turned out the light, and made his way upstairs. Elsie was still asleep. What a good job he hadn't wakened her. She would have ridiculed him unmercifully and got on to him for having left the light on. So he had better not say a word about it. Feeling pleased with himself at the satisfactory outcome of his little adventure, he carefully slid between the sheets and settled down once more to sleep.

And from behind the settee in the lounge, a badly scared burglar emerged, and pausing only to add the brass candlestick to the silver cups taken from the display cabinet, he let himself out through the French window.

A HOLIDAY ROMANCE

Nottingham
19.8.28.

Dear Marian,

I had a pleasant journey home from Blackpool on Saturday, thinking of you all the way. Already I am missing you and felt I must write straight away. We were lucky meeting on the first day of our holidays–I enjoyed every minute with you, particularly our last night after the concert. I do hope we shall correspond regularly and am looking forward to your letter as promised.

Love

Frank

Manchester
22.8.28.

Dear Frank,

I was delighted to receive your letter so soon. I too enjoyed our holiday and shall be pleased to keep up a correspondence. I've told Mum all about you and she says it is just a holiday romance and will soon pass off. I hope to prove her wrong! Yes, it is a pity we live so far from each other, but perhaps we could arrange to meet somewhere in between, what do you think? It would be nice to be together again.

Love

Marian

P. J. Barsby

Nottingham
26.8.28.

Dearest Marian,

It was good of you to reply so soon. It's a pity I haven't a car or there would be no problem. But I think it would be a good idea to meet somewhere in between, to save time travelling. What about Matlock, it's about halfway, I think. If you agree, I will make enquiries this end about trains from Nottingham, and perhaps you could enquire about trains from Manchester. Also about bus services. I still think about you every day and wonder what you are doing. So let me know how you spend your weekends and evenings, it will seem to bring us closer together.

All my love.

Frank

Manchester
30.8.28.

Dearest Frank,

I was thrilled to have your letter this morning, with your suggestion that we meet in Matlock. I am longing to see you again, dearest. Please do make enquiries about the trains and buses. I think the trains would be more convenient. You ask what I do at the weekends. Well, last weekend I went to the pictures with my friend Norah.

This weekend we have arranged to go to a dance, but I shall be thinking of you and wishing I was dancing with you.

All my love, darling.

Write soon.

Marian

Nottingham
2.9.28.

Dearest Marian,

I have now made enquiries regarding trains and buses to Matlock next Saturday. There is a train from Nottingham, with a change at Derby, arriving at Matlock at 3 pm. and a train from Manchester arriving about the same time, but please make enquiries regarding connections. It will be marvellous to see you again, darling, I just can't wait till Saturday.

Please let me know what you will be wearing so that I can easily recognise you. I shall be wearing a brown check sports jacket and grey flannels.

All my love.

Frank

Manchester
5.9.28.

Dearest Frank,

Thank you for the information about the trains. I too am getting excited at our meeting, and will be wearing a brown coat and hat. I will wait for you in the waiting room if you are not already there. Hope the weather keeps fine. It has been raining here as usual.

Until Saturday, darling.

All my love.

Marian

P. J. Barsby

Nottingham
16.9.28.

My darling Marian,

Wasn't it wonderful yesterday. You looked absolutely lovely and I love you more than ever. I was so sorry that I missed the connection at Derby through the train starting late from Nottingham, and that you had to wait an hour in the waiting room before I arrived. You must have thought I was never coming. Am glad we chose that nice little restaurant to have tea. I think the waitress must have guessed we were in love, she was so kind and attentive. Fancy you not liking marzipan, it's one of my favourites. It was so cosy just you and I being together in that little alcove. And weren't we fortunate in finding that quiet country lane and the field gate. Oh, you were absolutely wonderful. I hope you weren't disappointed in me but I just couldn't love you enough. We must meet again soon, my darling girl.

All my love.

Frank.

Manchester
18.9.28.

My dearest Frank,

Thank you for your lovely letter received this morning. I too enjoyed every minute of our meeting, and wasn't a bit disappointed in you, quite the reverse. It was heavenly being in your arms. We must find some way of meeting more often, I can't stand the strain of being without you. I feel too full to write more at present.

Love,

Marian

Nottingham
23. 9. 28.

Dearest Marian

I was glad to receive your letter of the 18th but sorry to hear you are feeling a bit down after our meeting. We really must try to meet again soon. What about you coming to Nottingham Goose Fair next month?

I believe there are excursions from Manchester, as we get thousands of visitors from other areas. Do please make enquiries, and if there is a suitable train and you can come, I will meet you off the train. Yesterday I went to the Nottm Forest v Blackpool match. Last Saturday we were together at Matlock. You can guess which I enjoyed the most!

I usually play football myself on Saturdays but we hadn't a match yesterday. What do usually do at the weekends? I think of you so often and wonder what you are doing.

All my love, dearest.

Frank

Manchester
27.9.28.

Dearest Frank

Your letter of the 23rd cheered me up no end. You ask what I do at the weekends. Well, last Saturday, the week after we were together in Matlock, I was actually in Blackpool, which brought back so many happy memories. There was an excursion and I went with my friend Nora.

We went on the Pleasure Beach on the South Shore, and went on the water slide and the chair-o-planes, and the dodgems, as you

P. J. Barsby

and I did together, and I couldn't help wishing you were with me again instead of Nora. Not that we don't get on well together, but you are so special.

I made enquiries about an excursion to Nottingham Goose Fair, and there is a train but my parents think the return train is far too late for me to be out. And now father has taken ill, so I am afraid it is off.

Love

Marian

Nottingham
7.10.28.

My dear Marian

Sorry I have been so long in replying to your last letter, but I have had a raging toothache. Eventually I went to the doctor and he found that there was an abcess under the tooth, so he couldn't take the tooth out until the abcess had burst. I have now had the tooth extracted but my face has swelled like a balloon, and I haven't felt like writing or doing anything. However, things are now more or less back to normal. What a co-incidence it was that you should be in Blackpool while I was watching Blackpool play Forest. I have been invited to join a concert party. They start rehearsals next week, so I will be able to tell you more about it in my next letter.

All my love as usual,

Frank

Manchester
4.11.28.

Dear Frank,

Sorry I was not able to make it to Goose Fair, but am pleased to say that Father has now fully recovered from his illness. The doctor suspected it was a slight heart attack and has advised father to take things easy. There's not much to report this time. I went to see Showboat with my friend Norah and it was a marvelous show. The singing was glorious.

Love,

Marian

Nottingham
19.11.28.

Dearest Marian,

I was very pleased to have your letter and to know that your father has fully recovered from his illness. It must have been a worrying time for you and your mother.

Our concert party gave its first concert in Derby last week. I had to learn the words of several songs, including "That's My Weakness Now", "I want to be alone with Mary Brown" and "The Sugar Step", which was our opening number, doing a sort of dance in line. It went down very well, and I didn't feel at all nervous, though it was the first time I have appeared on a public stage. We thought the concert would never take place, as the bus we had hired had a punctured front tyre when we were only halfway there. It took the driver twenty minutes to change the wheel, and by the time we got to Derby we had only a few minutes to spare. Then the driver, who was not sure of the way, asked how much further we had to go. It was then discovered we had passed the theatre and were entering Kedleston, the next village!

Eventually we found the theatre where anxious officials were waiting outside. We did a very quick change, and the curtain went up at 8.15, just a quarter of an hour late. But when the audience were

P. J. Barsby

told of our troubles, they gave us a cheer.

Looking forward to your next letter as always.

All my love,

Frank

Manchester
25.11.28.

Dear Frank,

Glad to hear that your first concert was a success, after your eventful ride. Now I hate to tell you this but I feel I must. For some time now I have been feeling that there is no future for our relationship. Because we live so far apart and seldom see each other and with no possibility of a change of circumstances, there seems no point in carrying on our friendship. Neither of us can be really happy with things as they are. I realised this when I went to a birthday party recently, where I danced with a boy I have known for some time.

Like you, he is a bit older than me, and like you has many of the qualities that attracted me to you. Since then, I have been out with him several times and have fallen in love with him.

I do hope you will see my point of view, and that you will soon find another girl who is more worthy of your love than I am. I shall never forget you, and thank you for all the pleasure you have given me.

Yours sincerely,

Marian

Nottingham
27.11.28.

Dearest Marian,

I was absolutely devastated and heartbroken to receive your letter. I love you with all my heart and could never find another girl like you. I know it is difficult not seeing much of each other, and I would willingly come to live in Manchester if there was any possibility of finding a job, but with the present unemployment this would be impossible. Also I have a very good job here.

To some extent I can understand your feelings, and if this is your wish I will not write again. But I cannot stop loving you, and if ever you find you have made a mistake, please don't hesitate to write and tell me.

All my love.

Frank

ALLOTMENT

It was just the right sort of afternoon for going on the allotment, sunny with a gentle cool breeze. I was very much behind with the work on my plot, what with evening meetings to attend, and bad weather when I hadn't. Funny how it always seems to rain when I have an evening free. So my main gardening activity was on Saturday afternoons, weather permitting. And today was ideal, so I planned the afternoon's work very carefully. I would set a row or two of peas in the part already dug, and perhaps a couple of rows of early potatoes before getting on with the digging.

When I arrived Old Bill was pottering about on his plot next to mine. He's a good gardener but he invariably stops work when I arrive and comes over for a chat, wasting an awful lot of time, or so it seems when one is busy. I had just begun to draw a drill for the peas when he came up from the other end of his plot.

"Good afternoon", he says cheerfully. "What are you putting in?"

"Peas" I said shortly.

"I can see that, but what kind are they?"

"Little Marvel", I replied, shorter still.

"Bit late this year, aren't you?"

"Yes".

"Lot of dock yonder in your plot", he continued.

"Yes, I'm going to clear it this afternoon, I hope", I said meaningly. Bill took the hint.

"Oh well, I'd better let you get on with it", he said.

"Yes, I've got a lot to do", I replied a little more graciously. And of he went to light a bonfire.

He doesn't consider he has had a good day's gardening unless he lights a bonfire, stands gazing at it, lights his pipe, and comes across to talk to anyone near him. How he gets his allotment done I don't know, except that he is retired and can put in the odd hour whenever he feels like it and the weather is suitable.

Anyway, I had just set a row of peas and covered them up when he comes up again.

"Have you seen my new greenhouse"? he began.

"Yes, I noticed it a fortnight ago. Did you have any difficulty in getting permission to have it erected?"

"Not really after they had seen the plans. Come across and have a look at it".

"Well, I'm rather busy", I began. " I've got lots of digging to do yet and I've got all that dock to get out". But he wouldn't' take no for an answer. "It won't take you a minute", he said pleadingly.

"All right", I replied without enthusiasm, and resigned myself to a further waste of time. Sullenly I walked with him to the other end of his plot. We looked at boxes and boxes of seedlings of various kinds and he was just like a boy with a new toy. We must have spent twenty minutes while he explained what the seedlings were and his preferences and prejudices.

Eventually I got away and had done about half an hour's work when he was back again, puffing away his pipe.

"Did you hear about the row between Brown and his wife", he began.

"No", I replied rather shortly. I didn't know the Browns very well and wasn't interested in any row they may have had. All I wanted to do was to concentrate on my allotment and the work which required doing. But Bill is a born story teller and it was ten minutes before he broke off to refill his pipe. I looked at my watch ostentatiously.

"Good heavens, it's four o'clock. I really must get on. Still got all this lot to dig".

"Yes, you are a bit behind" he said cheerfully. "Well, I suppose I must do a bit more". And back he went to potter about. Then it started to rain heavily. So I packed up for the afternoon, and still hadn't got the digging finished. Curse old Bill. I must have wasted a good hour listening to him and inspecting his greenhouse

I wasn't able to get on the allotment until the following Saturday afternoon. There was Old Bill pottering about as usual. Blast, I muttered. If he comes hindering me again I'll be rude to him. I had just time to hang my jacket on the post and roll up my sleeves when Bill came up.

"Good afternoon", he said in his usual cheerful manner.

"Afternoon", I replied shortly and rather ungraciously. I was in that sort of a mood.

"What are you going to do this afternoon?" he enquired.

"Digging", I replied grimly. "Must finish the digging this afternoon. Didn't seem to get on very well last week".

"You won't get any digging done this afternoon", said Bill.

"Why not?" I asked belligerently. "There'll be a row if I don't!"

"Well, see for yourself" said Bill, casually.

I looked down the allotment. It had all been dug and raked and was ready for setting.

"What's been going on?" I asked in amazement.

"Well" he began somewhat diffidently. "I saw you were a bit behind last week, so I thought I would finish it off for you. Hope you don't mind".

What with a feeling of bewilderment and a small lump in my throat, I could hardly speak. Here was I ready to curse Bill if he hindered me again, and he had evidently realised the predicament I was in and had unobtrusively set to and remedied the situation. And being the good gardener he was, he had made a better job of it than I could have done, and had removed all the dock.

"It's very good of you, Bill", I said at last. "And I'd like to repay you for your kindness".

"That's all right", he replied gruffly. He had already started hoeing. Then with a grin, "Mustn't waste time, or you'll never get those peas in!"

BLACKMAIL

Dawson Hague, the private detective, looked keenly at the young man sitting opposite. "You wish to see me on a confidential matter?"

"That's right. My name's Brown. I phoned you last night".

Hague noticed his client's agitated manner and the nervous way in which he lit a cigarette.

"I'm being blackmailed!" The young man took from his pocket an envelope and handed it to Hague.

"Just read that. It came yesterday".

Hague noticed that the envelope was postmarked Kensington and dated two days ago. It contained a single sheet of paper and a photograph. Hague glanced at the photograph before reading the letter. It was of a man and a girl in the nude, sitting up in bed. The man was undoubtedly his client. He read the letter, which was undated and bore no address.

Dear Mr. Brown,

I thought you might be interested to receive the enclosed photograph of a happy occasion. I think you will agree that it is a very good likeness, and I am also sure you will agree that your wife would be interested to see it. If you don't want this to happen, I will sell you the negative for £100. If you would like to meet me in the foyer of the Strand Palace Hotel at 8 o'clock next Friday, I will let you have the negative on payment of £100 in £5 notes. Carry a folded copy of the Evening Standard under your right arm for easy identification. If you do not come I will send a copy of the photograph to your wife.

There was no signature.

Hague glanced up. "Can you explain the photograph?"

Brown flushed. "I'd better begin at the beginning", he said.

"Two months ago I came to London on a three day business conference. I had just left my hotel one evening when a girl passing by seemed to stumble. I asked her if she was all right, and she said, "I've twisted my ankle, I think. I wonder if you would mind calling me a taxi. I live in Kensington". So I called a taxi and felt in honour bound I should see her home. She was a very attractive girl, and this may have influenced my decision. On the way she told me she lived alone in a flat and worked in an office in the City. When we arrived at her flat, she invited me in for a drink. I remembered later that her ankle had seemed less painful when we got out of the taxi, as she walked up the steps of the building without limping. The flat was nicely furnished and tastefully decorated. She offered me a glass of sherry. Later we had whiskey and I don't mind telling you I got rather sozzled and amorous. So did she. In the end, we got into bed together, and, well, you can guess the rest". He paused.

"Who took the photograph?", asked Hague.

"I don't know. There must have been someone in the next room with a camera focused on the bed. I remember we sat up as I thought I heard a slight sound from the wall opposite, but the girl said I imagined it as there was no one else in the flat. I think now that the whole thing was planned, and that someone is in league with the girl, getting her to entice men to the flat, then

P. J. Barsby

photographing them in compromising situations for blackmail purposes".

"How did she know your name and address?"

"Well, I remember I felt drowsy after making love, and dozed off. Perhaps one of the drinks was drugged. She could have looked in my wallet".

"Have you been to the police?"

"No, I don't want it to get out if I can help it. I thought you might advise me privately".

"What was the address the girl took you to?"

"Flat 8, Kensington Court".

"Would you recognise the girl again?"

"I'm almost sure I would. She had a mole on her left cheek".

"You don't know her name?"

"No".

"Excuse me a moment". Dawson Hague picked up a telephone directory and dialled a number.

"Electoral Registration Officer?"

"Speaking".

"Can you give me the name of the occupant of Flat Number 8. Kensington Court? I'm trying to trace someone".

"Just a moment". After a few seconds delay, the voice replied,

"The flat is occupied by Arthur Hampson and Catherine Hampson".

"Thanks a lot". Hague jotted the names on a pad. Turning to his client, he said

"The girl told you she lived alone?"

"That's right".

"Well, according to the electoral registration officer the flat is occupied by Arthur Hampson and Catherine Hampson. If they are working a racket between them, I think we can find out. Now, listen carefully. I want you to keep the appointment and take the £100 in £5 notes as requested. Ask your bank for consecutive numbers if possible and keep a note of all the numbers. I shall be in the foyer of the Strand Palace in disguise when you arrive. When you have paid over the money and got the negative, go straight back home and I will phone you later".

On Friday evening, Brown walked into the foyer of the hotel, carrying a folded copy of the Evening Standard under his right arm as directed. There were two people at the reception desk and three or four standing chatting. On a settee sat a bearded man with tinted spectacles reading an evening paper, and sitting next to him was a tall man who looked directly at Brown. The man rose and came over to him. "Mr. Brown?"

"That's right". Brown noticed that the man was smartly dressed in a dark suit, with a plain blue shirt and striped tie. He had wavy hair and looked to be in his early thirties.

"I trust you have brought the cash?"

"Yes, here it is". Brown handed over an envelope containing the notes. Hampson counted them carefully and put them in his wallet. Then he produced a slim envelope "Here's the negative."

Brown held it up to the light. It showed two people sitting up in bed, but it was difficult to tell whether it was him and the girl.

"Don't worry. It's the negative you wanted", the man said.

"I wouldn't double-cross you. You need worry no more". He stood up.

"Nice to have met you". And he walked out through the swing doors. Rather disappointed at not having seen the detective, Brown left the hotel and drove straight home. At the same time the man with the beard and tinted spectacles followed Hampson out of the hotel and to the Underground, where Hampson took a ticket for Kensington. Had he turned round when he entered Flat No.8 Kensington Court, he would have seen a man with a beard and tinted spectacles walking by. And he would have been very uneasy had he known that the little black case the man was carrying contained a tape recording of his conversation in the foyer of the hotel.

The next morning, Hague phoned his friend Inspector Baker of Scotland Yard.

"Hello, Inspector. Have you anything on your files about Arthur Hampson of Flat 8, Kensington Court?"

"I'll check up. In the meantime, what's the trouble?"

"I've reason to believe he's running a blackmail racket from the flat, enticing men into the flat and then photographing them in compromising situations with his wife or girl friend. I would like you to come over and listen to a tape recording I've made".

"Okay. Shall we say eight o'clock this evening? Oh, by the way, we've got nothing on Hampson".

At eight o'clock Inspector Baker sat with Hague listening to the tape recording.

"I'm afraid that's not enough evidence on its own to take proceedings", said the Inspector. "But this letter from Hampson is distinctive". He picked up the letter and read it again.

"The small 'e' on the typewriter is out of alignment".

"Yes, I noticed that", said Hague. "And I think that will help us in our enquiries. My plan is this. My assistant will pose as a salesman for Photographic Supplies Limited. He will call at the flat, offering to supply films at wholesale prices. By this ruse he should gain admittance to the flat, and hopefully may see the photographic equipment. And he may possibly find out where the camera is operated. He will also try to obtain evidence that the typewriter has a faulty 'e'. If we can collect sufficient evidence, then I suggest you obtain a warrant to search the flat".

"Seems a good idea". Inspector Baker took out a notebook. "Is your assistant known to the Hampsons?"

"No, that's why I suggest he goes in the first place. I'll give you a ring as soon as he gets back".

The next day, a young man rang the bell at the flat and waited.

The door was opened by an attractive woman in her early thirties.

"Good afternoon", began the young man who was Hague's assistant.

"I represent Direct Photographic Supplies Limited. We supply films at wholesale prices. Are you interested in photography?"

"Well, I am not but my husband is. He's not in at present. Perhaps you could call later - he should be back about six o'clock".

"Thanks. I'll call again this evening."

At six o'clock Tommy Brook, Hague's assistant, returned to the flat and was admitted. Mr. Hampson proved to be a keen and knowledgeable photographer who did his own developing and printing. Yes, he would certainly like to buy films at wholesale prices. He used a 35 mm Pentax with interchangeable lenses, and had a small darkroom. "I'd love to see your darkroom", said Brook. I'm thinking of doing my own developing and printing and would like some tips". All unsuspectingly Hampson showed Brook the darkroom, which was situated off the bedroom. Brook expressed his interest and pleasure in the equipment he saw, which included an enlarger.

"Thanks for showing me your equipment. I'll arrange for a supply of films to be posted to you. I wonder if your typist would type out the order for me. I've forgotten to bring any invoice forms". The young woman obligingly typed out the order, and Brook took his departure, after noting with satisfaction the mis-aligned 'e' on the typewritten sheet.

The next day, Dawson Hague called on Inspector Baker and showed him the typed order.

"You will see that the type-face on the order corresponds with that on the letter sent to my client. It would seem from what my assistant tells me, that the darkroom adjoins the bedroom, and that a camera could be focused on the bed, possibly through a hole in a thin partition".

Inspector examined the order and the blackmail letter. "Yes, there's no doubt it is the same typewriter. I will get a search warrant".

When the flat was searched, it was found that the darkroom was indeed partitioned off from the bedroom by a screen in which a hole had been drilled, through which the camera was operated. Sufficient evidence having been obtained, Hampson was prosecuted for his blackmailing activities, and duly sent to prison.

And Dawson Hague's client vowed that never again would he be duped by an attractive woman.

BLUE EYED GIRL

"Say goodnight to Daddy!" I presented our two children to my husband for their goodnight kiss, after bathing them and putting on their pyjamas. George gave John a hug and a kiss, but looked strangely at Carol giving her a perfunctory kiss on the forehead.

When I came downstairs after putting the children to bed, he sat with his head in his hands, looking dejected.

"What's the matter, George?", I asked.

In a strained voice, he replied, "You know very well what's the matter, Margaret", he replied.

"I don't know what you are talking about. What's come over you? You've been very surly for some time now. Is anything worrying you?" His reply stunned me.

"I've suspected for some time that you've been unfaithful to me, and that Carol isn't my child. Now I've proof!"

Whatever was he saying? He had been a bit edgy and morose for weeks but I thought it was his job getting him down as he had been on overtime. We had been married for four years and had been reasonably happy until the past few weeks. Our son John was born just a year after we were married, and George had doted on him. Then Carol came along. She was a lovely baby with deep blue eyes. George had remarked on the colour, as both of us have brown eyes. We felt that they might change colour but they remained a vivid blue. George now sat with his head down and a look of utter dejection on his face.

I couldn't believe what he was saying. Before I had met George, I had been going steady with Mark, who worked in our office. His fair curly hair and vivid blue eyes in a tanned face made him attractive. He was very passionate in his love making and wanted to go all the way, but I told him firmly no, and if he persisted I wouldn't see him again. And I deliberately avoided him for a fortnight.

Then I heard he was going out with Florrie in the dispatch office. At first I was jealous and began to wonder whether I ought to have let him do as he wanted. But I was glad later on that I hadn't.

Feeling lonely one evening after hearing about Mark and Florrie, I went to a dance at the Masonic Hall. I just couldn't bear to stay in on my own. And it was at this dance that I met George. He too was on his own, and he asked me for a dance. We danced together perfectly and afterwards he came and sat with me. He seemed a few years old than I and rather serious, the type who would be dependable. He was in every way different from Mark. He had dark brown hair and lovely warm brown eyes; and the fact that he was older seemed to make him more attractive.

We met frequently after that evening, and soon I was head over heels in love with him. We became engaged, and a year later were married. We were both very happy when our son John was born, and eighteen months later when I told George that I was pregnant again, he seemed quite pleased. "Let's hope for a lovely girl this time, like you", he said.

It was in the early stages of my pregnancy that I went out shopping leaving John with my neighbour. The weather had turned cold, and it started to drizzle, so I went in a cafe on the High Street to have a coffee to warm me up. I found an empty table and sat down. And then I saw him.

Mark was sitting at the next table, and our eyes met. He smiled and came across.

"Nice to see you again", he said. My heart seemed to miss a beat.

"Mind if I sit with you?"

"Please do". Somehow I felt embarrassed and yet flattered. I hadn't seen him since we parted, at least not to speak to, and the memory of our last meeting was still quite vivid.

"Well, how's life treating you?" His voice appeared casual. I told him I was happily married, and asked him how he was faring.

"Oh, I'm still single". He hesitated a moment, then said "You know I shall never find another girl like you. I was a fool, but well, I loved you but just couldn't control my feelings. But there it is", he ended, trying to appear cheerful. I was embarrassed and didn't know what to say.

"Have you any children?", he asked, after a pause. I told him about John, and that I was expecting another child. After that there seemed nothing much to talk about. Sensing my embarrassment, he made a show of looking at his wrist-watch.

"Well, I really must be going, but it's been nice having a chat with you again. I shall never forget you, Margaret. All the very best to you and your family". And he walked slowly out of the cafe, not even turning round at the door, as I half expected him to.

For some days afterwards I couldn't get him out of my mind. I could see his blue eyes smiling at me in that quizzical, half-bantering way, and kept thinking of what might have been. But I was now happily married, and I resolutely put away all thoughts of him. Could it be, though, that my thoughts of his blue eyes had somehow caused my child to have such vivid blue eyes? No, it was too ridiculous to think of I was jolted back to the present by George speaking again.

"I didn't mention it to you at the time because I thought little of it then, but you were seen having tea with Mark Tapley at the Oxford Restaurant some months ago. Now I understand. No doubt you have been having several little cosy meetings since then. Everyone knows he is out for what he can get, you told me so yourself and said that was why you gave him up. When we became engaged, you said you had completely put him out of your mind, but it's obvious you've been seeing him secretly since our marriage, and no doubt you've let him seduce you.

"It's pretty obvious where Carol gets her blue eyes from!"

I felt sick in the stomach at George's unfounded allegations.

He had been very jealous of my association with Mark when we became engaged, but I thought he had got over it when we got married. Someone must have told him of our chance meeting in the cafe and put the worst construction on it. So that was the reason for George's moroseness during the past few weeks, brooding over my supposed infidelity, and keeping it all to himself.

Somehow, in spite of my initial anger at his allegations, I felt sorry for him.

"Oh, George!" I threw my arms round him. "Why didn't you tell me what's been troubling you? That visit to the cafe is the only time I've seen Mark to speak to since we were married. I was out shopping, and went into the Oxford restaurant for a coffee, and he happened to be sitting at the next table. He came across and had a chat, that's all. It was quite a co-incidence and I've never seen him since. I didn't mention it to you at the time because I thought it might make you unnecessarily jealous".

Editor's note: The following is a fragment found on the computer. It appears that this story was never quite finished.

"Then why is it that Carol has blue eyes and fair hair, yet both of our families are dark?"

"I don't know, George, I really don't. But I know I love you and you alone, and have never been unfaithful to you". And I broke down and cried.

Then I felt George's arms round me.

"I'm sorry, darling", he said, and kissed me tenderly. "I've nearly been out of my mind having these suspicions". He squeezed me tight. "Please forgive me for all the rotten things I've said". We clung to each other, but somehow I felt he still had a lingering doubt.

A few weeks later I had a letter from my Grandma Bentley to tell me she had come to live in an old people's home at Langford only a few miles from where we were living, and inviting us to go over and see her and bring the children.

At first, George didn't want to go, but ever since his outburst he had tried hard to please me. Seeing my look of disappointment, he quickly said, "Oh, all right, we'll go next week".

CONFERENCE CAMEO

With purposeful steps he mounted the rostrum. A hush fell on the vast assembly. Gazing down on the sea of faces below, he waved his agenda paper.

"Mr. Chairman, fellow delegates", he began. And then followed an amazing spate of oratory. Clear, concise, forceful, he marshalled his facts and dealt with the points raised by the previous speaker. There was no doubt he had made a hit. He visualised headlines in the morning papers, followed by a verbatim report of his important speech.

As he stepped down from the rostrum, conscious of having made a masterly speech, he was dimly aware of the tremendous burst of clapping as he made his way back to his seat. Arms seemed to be outstretched towards him, anxious to congratulate him on his outstanding speech. Someone slapped him on the back. "Wake up", said a voice in his ear. "You've just missed the best speech of the conference!"

CRISIS ONE [*]

He had felt somewhat embarrassed and didn't know what to say next. Being so near the girl seemed to put a spell on him. After a slight hesitation, he had said, "May I sit with you a moment?"

"Please do". She indicated a seat beside her, and soon he was chatting with them like old friends. He learned that her name was Hazel and that her mother was a widow. Hazel had contracted polio at an early age and had been somewhat incapacitated ever since. There was not a trace of bitterness or self pity as they recounted the shock when the disease struck. In fact, they made light of their troubles, and the mother courteously enquired about Trevor. He gave them a brief account of his rather uneventful life, then the conversation seemed to flag.

"What are you doing this evening?", he asked, more for something to say than anything else.

"Well, we haven't really decided", replied Hazel. "We were thinking of going to the Follies on the pier".

"So was I", he had lied on the spur of the moment. "Would you think it presumptuous if I suggested we went together? I'm on my own and it would be nice to make up a party".

Hazel looked at her mother who smiled pleasantly. "It's very nice of you to offer, but we don't want to spoil your evening, you know"

It didn't. They went to see the Follies, and Trevor sat next to Hazel, with her mother on the other side. During the show, he had tentatively put his arm round Hazel's waist and was not rebuffed.

In fact, he felt an answering pressure on his arm.

CRISIS TWO

Trevor Brown looked at the envelope with a puzzled expression. It bore a London postmark and was addressed in unfamiliar hand-writing. Pushing a thumb in the flap, he opened the envelope and drew out the letter. It was from Mrs. Weston to say that her daughter Hazel was seriously ill. She had been calling Trevor's name in her delirium, and Mrs. Weston wondered whether it would be possible for him to come and see her and perhaps help in her recovery.

As he read the letter, memories came flooding back of the holiday he had spent at Llandudno last year. He had met her at the hotel on the first night of his holiday. It was her eyes that had attracted him in the first place, lovely dark eyes with a hint of sadness. She was sitting at a corner table in the dining room with a middle-aged person he learned later was her mother.

The girl appeared to be in her late twenties, but there were tiny lines at the corners of her mouth as though she had suffered. But this only seemed to give character to a face that was tranquil, yet with this hint of sadness.

He remembered how embarrassed he had felt when she looked up and caught him staring at her. He had smiled rather self-consciously to cover his embarrassment, and she had smiled back, a rather wistful smile which lit up her face like sunshine chasing away clouds.

He felt he must make her acquaintance, and wondered whether she would be keen on dancing. There was a dance at the hotel that evening, and it would be a good opportunity to get introduced. She looked the kind of girl who would dance divinely. He visualised himself going up to her and asking her for a waltz. She would smile graciously in acceptance, and already he could feel her pressed close to him, swaying in perfect rhythm to the lilting music of the waltz in the dimly lit ballroom.

Afterwards they would go for a walk on the promenade and listen to the murmur of the sea and watch the moonlight glittering on the waves. He remembered every detail of that evening. How, after the meal, he had glanced at her again, and how devastatingly beautiful she was. As if knowing she was being watched, she had looked across and caught his eye. They had both smiled, and he felt as though a bond had been forged between them. And then, shortly afterwards, the two women had risen from their seats. The younger one appeared to have some difficulty in getting up from the table. After sliding sideways, she stood up. He remembered the shock when he saw that her right leg was in a caliper. As she walked ungainly by, she gave him a wistful smile. His thoughts went back to the dance they were going to have, the dreamy waltz under the soft lights of the ballroom.

Something welled up in his throat. He smiled back with what he hoped was a comforting smile. Now he knew the reason for the sad look in those beautiful eyes. Not for her the joys of dancing or tennis or swimming in the sea. Just a patient life with a devoted mother. He had gone up to his room in a thoughtful frame of mind. He was on his own, fancy free, and hoped to find a pretty girl to share his holiday pleasures. She would have been the ideal girl but for her infirmity. He remembered how, as he came down the stairs, she and her mother were sitting in the lounge. She had smiled her lovely smile, and on an impulse he had stopped and said, "Isn't the weather marvellous?" "It is". Again that wondrous smile. "Let's hope it stays like it"!

After the show, he escorted them back to the hotel, and Hazel and her mother thanked him for a pleasant evening. They had booked to go on a day trip in the morning, and excused themselves for retiring early. The next day Trevor felt quite lost without their company, and eagerly looked forward to their return in the evening. He met them in the lounge after dinner.

"Had a good day?", he enquired.

"Yes, very pleasant". Hazel looked at him with a smile.

"Did you have a nice day?"

"Not so bad, but not so nice as last evening", he had replied.

And he remembered that Hazel had blushed.

The three of them spent the remaining days of the holiday together, and he promised to write to Hazel when he got home. They did in fact correspond for a few months, but gradually there was a longer interval between the letters. And Trevor had not replied to her last letter though he had intended to.

Somehow, the aura of the holiday had worn off. There was her infirmity which subconsciously he supposed, had put him off, and his hobby of photography occupied a great deal of his time. He felt rather guilty when he remembered that he had not replied to her last letter, though he had fully intended to. And now this letter had come.

At first he was undecided what to do. He could write and express his sympathy, and offer her his sincere wishes for a speedy recovery. Or he could visit her. He picked up the letter and read it again. Between the lines he sensed it was a cry from the heart. He decided he would go, and as he did so, he had a strange feeling that he was making a momentous decision. If he didn't go and Hazel died, he would have it on his conscience for the rest of his life.

There was an hourly rail service from his home in the Midlands, and the journey would take two hours. After wiring Mrs. Weston that he would be there late in the afternoon, he arranged with the office have the afternoon off.

On the journey down, he began to wonder whether he had done the right thing. After all, the holiday romance had worn off and he didn't really want to get involved again. But at least he would have a clear conscience if the worst happened.

When he arrived at Hazel's home - a pleasant semi-detached house in a tree-lined avenue, Mrs. Weston answered his knock. "I'm so glad you've come, it's very kind of you", she greeted him as she led him into the house. "Hazel has been calling your name so many times", and she sobbed uncontrollably.

"Please don't cry", said Trevor. "I'm sure things will be all right".

Dabbing her eyes with a tiny handkerchief, Mrs. Weston preceded him into the bedroom where Hazel lay. He was shocked by her appearance. Her sunken cheeks were flushed, and there was an unnatural stare in those lovely eyes. He felt terribly inadequate.

"Hello Hazel", he said. "I'm sorry you are so poorly", and then he couldn't think of anything else to say. She stared at him with a puzzled expression.

"Do you remember the holiday we had at Llandudno?", he asked gently.

And then recognition seemed to come to her. "Trevor", she breathed, and lapsed into unconsciousness. Mrs. Weston and Trevor spoke in whispers.

She told him that the doctor had said that the crisis could be expected this evening, and that he would be calling later.

"I think we'd better have a cup of tea. I'm sure you could do with one". Mrs. Weston looked at him enquiringly.

"Well, I wouldn't mind if you are having one yourself", he replied. The rattle of crockery seemed to waken Hazel. She stirred, and then sat up. After looking rather wildly round the room, she saw Trevor, and smiled.

"How do you feel, darling?", he asked.

"Much better, thank you. Please stay a little longer. You do me good". And she smiled her lovely smile.

Trevor knew at that moment that not only had the crisis passed for Hazel, but that the conflict in his mind had been resolved and that he really loved this girl who had captivated him on holiday.

Shortly afterwards, the doctor came, and confirmed that the crisis had passed. He was amazed at the improvement in her condition since his previous visit.

As Mrs. Weston took the doctor downstairs, Hazel turned to Trevor and said, "I owe my life to you, Trevor. You have given me the will to live" and her eyes filled with tears. "I don't know how I can ever repay you for your kindness". "I do". Trevor's voice was husky with emotion. "By becoming my wife and making me the happiest man in the world". Her outstretched arms left no doubt what her answer would be.

DIAMONDS ARE A GIRL'S BEST FRIEND

She hummed a little tune as she stood at the sink, preparing for lunch. Her husband wouldn't be home until one o'clock and there was time for a cup of coffee before she put the saucepan on. A slight sound behind her caused her to turn round. A man stood watching her, a small bag in his hand. She was terrified.

"What are you doing here?", she asked.

"I want your money", the man replied".

"I haven't got any money in the house", she whimpered

"Then I'll have your jewellery", he snarled as he gripped her by the throat with his massive hands. As his grip tightened, she wished she had learned Judo or King Fu or any of the martial arts. There was some way of beating a man who held you by the throat.

"Come on", said the man, pressing her throat tighter. "Show me where your jewels are quick, or you're a goner".

Then she thought of the diamond ring on her left hand. Clenching her fist, she quickly raised her arm and brought the back of her fist smartly down on the man's face. The diamond cut deeply into the skin and made a nasty gash, from which the blood spurted. The man released his grip and put his hand to his face. As he did so, she grabbed a heavy saucepan and brought it smartly down on his head. He crumpled up and slid to the floor.

Trembling, she picked up the phone and dialled 999. And as she waited, the words of the song drifted through her head. Diamonds are a girl's best friend.

GOOD DOG, SCAMP!

Miss Travalga was beginning to get worried. Her mongrel terrier was missing. Someone had left the garden gate open and apparently Scamp had wandered off. But it was most unusual for him to stay out so long. She had had him six years, and a more intelligent and lovable dog would be hard to find. He understood his mistress's every movement, obeyed her every wish, and generally did his best to show what a pleased little fellow he was.

Her thoughts were interrupted by a knock on the door. Mechanically she opened the door, thinking it was probably the butcher's boy. A man stood outside, and in his arms was Scamp, blood coming from his mouth, and glazed look in his eyes.

Scamp dead! Miss Travalga's heart seemed to miss a beat.

"I'm sorry, but I've knocked your dog down. Another dog was chasing him and he ran in front of my car. I was going very slowly as I could see what was likely to happen. The bumper caught him, but I don't think he is badly hurt".

"Oh, my poor dear Scamp", murmured Miss Travalga, fighting to keep the tears from her eyes. "please bring him in".

The man washed the blood from Scamp's mouth and skillfully bound up the damaged paw.

"There, old man. You'll soon be all right". Turning to Miss Travalga, he said "If you feel you'd like to take him to the vet for a check up, I'll be pleased to pay the bill. But I think his wound is only superficial, and he should be all right in a day or two". He picked up his hat.

"Won't you stay for a cup of tea, Mr. ....?

"Brown's the name. It's very kind of you, but I really must be going. But I'll call tomorrow to see how the invalid is getting on".

Scamp feebly wagged his tail as though he understood what was being said, and thoroughly approved.

Miss Travalga watched the man's retreating figure as he walked down the garden path. She liked his sturdy shoulders and manly bearing. He didn't look back. When news of Scamp's accident got round the village, many of the neighbours called to express their sympathy. All the villagers loved Miss Travalga. She was so kind and sympathetic to everyone in their troubles. Always bright and cheerful, her life's mission seemed to be to brighten other people's lives. And in this she succeeded. All the neighbours thought what a happy and contented person Miss Travalga was. But they were wrong.

Before coming to live in the village, Miss Travalga had looked after her widowed mother who was crippled with arthritis. When she died, she left her life's savings to her daughter, with which Miss Travalga had bought a cottage in the village. She was now in her late fifties, and opportunities for marriage had passed her by. So she lavished all her love and devotion on Scamp, who fully appreciated all the fuss and attention.

The next morning, Miss Travalga felt strangely happy. Was it because Scamp had practically fully recovered from the accident, or was it because Mr. Brown had said he would call to see how Scamp was getting on? And was that why she had put on her nicest dress, the one she seldom wore because there was no one to see her in it, except the neighbours, and they preferred her in her homely, everyday wear.

The day wore on but Mr. Brown had not come. Dozens of times during the day Miss Travalga glanced at the clock. Of course, she really wasn't expecting him until late afternoon. That was why she put on the best tablecloth and got out her best tea service.

Four o'clock. She decided she would have a later tea today. Four thirty. Five o'clock.

There came a knock at the door. Miss Travalga's heart gave a flutter, and a becoming flush stole over her sweet features. She went to the door. Yes, it was he. "Do come in, Mr. Brown". He stepped inside.

"And how's the patient? Getting on very nicely? He was pleased to hear that. Yes, it was very kind of her, he would stay to tea.

Miss Travalga looked positively pretty and even younger in her happiness. One of the happiest teatimes in her recollection followed. Mr. Brown was a most interesting man in every way. Kind. Quietly humorous. A retired naval captain. Unmarried. Miss Travalga's romantic heart beat as it had seldom beaten before.

When, after an hour's interesting conversation, Mr. Brown rose to go he promised he would look in again in a few days.

He came the next week, and the week after, and soon became a regular visitor. And then, when he came one day and stayed on after tea, he asked her somewhat shyly if she would like to become Mrs. Brown. A great joy bounded in her heart. She could hardly whisper "Yes such a flood of feeling welled up in her. Tenderly, Mr. Brown put his arms round her, and she lay with her head against the rough tweed of his jacket, sobbing gently through sheer happiness.

The ever faithful Scamp sensed his mistress's happiness. Putting his front paws on her knees, he gazed enquiringly at her. Drying her eyes, Miss Travalga stooped down and gave Scamp a hug. "Good dog, Scamp!", she said. And Mr. Brown, realising it was solely due to Scamp that they had both found true happiness, patted his head and repeated with fervour, "Good dog, Scamp!"

HAPPY FACES

George White couldn't sleep. He lay tossing and turning, his mind fully awake, as his wife lay peacefully beside him. His thoughts turned to the New Year, only three days away. The past year had been quite successful; he had been promoted in the office, and his bank balance was quite healthy. But somehow he felt dissatisfied.

For one thing, he didn't get the respect he felt was his due. His wife treated him coldly at times, and the office staff resented his frequent outbursts when things went wrong. Perhaps it was his own fault. He admitted to himself that he hadn't shown any affection for his wife lately, and he did go off the deep end at times when work piled up at the office.

He gazed at his wife sleeping so peacefully. Poor dear, he thought. I haven't really treated her well during the past year. How many times have I taken her out? Hardly at all, except for the cricket club dance and the darts club dinner. How often have I shown her that I still care? Not very often. Poor Mildred. I really ought to be more considerate.

His thoughts turned again to the New Year. Now was the time to make new resolutions. Yes, he would be more loving to his wife, and more kindly and considerate to his colleagues in the office. In fact he would be kind to everyone. And another thing. he really ought to take some exercise. He was getting quite corpulent round the middle, and a little bit out of breath at the least exertion.

With these thoughts in mind, he drifted off to sleep. In the morning he remembered his resolutions of the night before. True, it wasn't yet the New Year, but there was no harm in having a dummy run. Glancing at his watch, he saw that it was only 7.30,

and usually he didn't get up till eight. But now was the time.
Quietly slipping out of bed, he made his way to the bathroom. He
would wash and shave, do five minutes stretch and bend, then take
Mildred a cup of tea, a thing he hadn't done for years. She would
be pleased.

Stretching his arms above his head, he bent down to touch his toes.
There came the sound of tearing cloth as his pyjamas refused to
bear the unusual strain, and it suddenly seemed chilly round
Piccadilly Circus. But he persevered, stretching and bending until
an agonising pain shot through his groin. That's enough for today,
anyway, he thought as he limped from the bathroom to the kitchen,
where he made a cup of tea.

His wife was still asleep, and he bent down gently to waken her.
As he did so, the cup slithered in the saucer, and his wife wakened
with a yell as the hot tea splashed on her nightie. She jumped up in
alarm. "What on earth are you playing at?", she asked, dabbing at
her nightie with a handkerchief.

"I've just brought you a cup of tea, dear, that's all", he replied with
as much dignity as he could muster.

"What's come over you?", asked Mildred. "I don't mind a cup of
tea in bed but I don't want scalding!" And with a bad grace she
sipped the tea. Immediately she pulled a face. "UGH!", she
grumbled, "You've put sugar in it and you know I don't take
sugar!"

"Sorry dear, I forgot", he apologised. "I'll make you another cup".

"Don't bother", said Mildred. "It's time to get up anyway. What
are you limping for?"

"Oh, I slipped in the bathroom. Nothing to worry about".

In the evening, George arrived home with a box of soft-centred chocolates.

"What's that you've got?", asked Mildred.

"Just a box of chocolates for you, dear", he replied, handing them to her. Mildred looked at him with suspicion.

"What's all this in aid of?"

"Nothing. Just a New Year's present", he said shyly.

"Now what are you after?", asked Mildred.

"Nothing", replied George with dignity. "I was just passing the sweet shop on the way home and I thought you might like a box of chocolates".

"Well, thanks all the same, but you know I'm on a diet and don't eat chocolates".

"Oh well, it was just a thought. You can offer them to your friends when they call".

Mildred put down the chocolates and looked at George suspiciously.

"Are you feeling all right?"

"Of course I am".

George was beginning to wish he hadn't bought the chocolates. His New Year resolution didn't seem to be working out too well and he felt rather a fool.

At the office next morning, Elaine the typist brought in the letters for signing. As he read them, George noticed the usual typing errors and miss-spelt words. He really couldn't allow the letters to go out like this. But he must curb his temper and not shout at the poor girl as he usually did. He pressed the bell.

Elaine came in with a sulky expression on her face. She resented being ticked off, though she knew it was her own fault. "Oh, Elaine. Do you mind doing these two letters again. I've changed my mind and altered then a bit". Elaine took the letters open mouthed. Back in her office, she confided to her colleague Mary that there was something funny about the boss. "He was actually nice to me and never said anything about the mistakes I had made in the letters. Said it was his own fault they had to be typed again".

"You'd better watch out" said Mary. "Perhaps he has designs on you. You know what these middle-aged men are like. Don't they call it the seven year itch or something. Anyway, if he makes a pass at you just kick him on the shins. That will stop any of his little tricks!".

In the Dog and Duck that evening, George had just ordered his usual pint when Freddie Forbes came in. He was a member of the darts team.

"What are you having?", asked George.

Freddie looked at him in surprise. It was the first time he had ever known George to offer to buy a drink without being treated first.

"I'll have half a mild, if you don't mind", he said. Soon the news got round the darts team that George was up to something - "buying drinks, right, left and centre". Was he currying favour for the captaincy, they wondered. Better watch him. There's something fishy going on .

At the weekend, George remembered that his wife didn't eat chocolates, so he decided to buy her a bunch of flowers.

"What have you got there?", Mildred enquired when he arrived home.

"Oh, nothing. Just a few flowers for you, dear".

"Whatever for? You haven't bought any flowers since your Dad's funeral".

"Well, I thought it might brighten the house up a bit".

"Oh, so you think the house needs brightening up, do you. Don't I slave enough all week to keep it nice and tidy, while you leave all your things lying about."

"Sorry dear, I'll try to me more tidy in future", he replied meekly. But all the joy of giving her the flowers had gone completely His New Year resolutions didn't seem to be going at all well. It was only the first week, and already his wife was suspicious of his intentions; the office staff thought he had gone crazy, and the darts team eyed him with pitying glances, as though he was sickening for something.

All right, blow them. He had tried to make a fresh start but it seemed that nobody appreciated it. He would be his usual self again and they could like it or lump it.

But it wasn't so easy. When Elaine brought the letters in next day, she had a smile on her face, probably remembering how nice he had been when she had made the mistakes. George noticed for the first time how pretty she looked when she smiled. And when he read the letters and found no mistakes, he called her in and congratulated her on the neatness of her typing. She blushed, and both were happy. He liked the feeling that had now come over him. And when Thomas the junior brought in the tea, George smiled and asked him if he had had a nice weekend.

"Yes, sir, thank you. I made fifty not out on Saturday, playing for the village team".

"Good for you", replied George. "I can see you playing for England yet", and smiled.

"Thank you, sir", replied Thomas, and withdrew with a happy smile on his face.

George picked up the intercom to the main office. "Will you ask Mr. Forbes to come in for a moment".

Freddie Forbes was the secretary of the darts club, and was somewhat surprised to be ushered into the boss's office.

"Sit down, Fred", said George. "I've been thinking about the darts team. I wish to present a trophy, and would like your advice. I thought perhaps a challenge trophy to be awarded annually, but think it over and let me know what would be acceptable, after talking it over with the members". Freddie rose.

"It's very good of you. I'm sure the members will be delighted with your suggestion." And he took his departure with a smile on his face. George felt a warm glow at the friendship. When he got home, Mildred said, "You seem very pleased with yourself. Have you had some luck?"

"Yes dear", replied George. I've realised how lucky I am to have you, and to have so many friends. Let's go out tonight and celebrate".

Mildred flung her arms round George and hugged him. Smiling through her tears, she said, "That's the nicest thing I've heard for a long time. I feel so happy".

And for the first time for months, George felt happy too.

HIGHWAYMAN SILVER RING

I awakened, bathed in perspiration. It was some seconds before I realised I had been dreaming, everything seemed so real. Eventually I dozed off.

In the morning the dream remained so vivid that I walked back to the road where I had found myself in my dream last night. Yes, there was the bush that I had stood behind, and there was the clump of trees behind which the highwayman had concealed himself. And opposite was the tree where one of the ladies had dropped her ring. I searched for some time but found nothing except a few pieces of flint and some stones.

All that day I had the feeling that my dream really happened, so at the weekend I went back to the tree with a small trowel. I scraped away the dead leaves and dug among the roots, carefully sifting the soil. But after ten minutes without finding anything I decided to give it up. It must have been a dream, after all. And then I saw something. It turned out to be a dirty blackened ring.

My heart thumped with excitement as I scraped the soil from it but it was in poor condition so I took it home and gave it a thorough clean in hot soapy water. It was a silver ring, and on the inside was engraved To E.S. from G.S. 21st May 1739.

STRANGE ENCOUNTER

The scudding clouds dappled the moonlit road with mysterious shadows, and the countryside seemed very peaceful as I walked along.

Suddenly, the stillness was broken by the sound of horses hooves clip-clopping on the road. This was rather surprising as it was after midnight. Somehow I felt a sense of foreboding, and instinctively hid behind a tree near the side of the road. The sound of the horse's hooves became louder, and there came into sight a horseman riding a black horse. The rider was dressed in a long black cloak with a high collar, and on his head was a tri-corn hat edged with gold braiding. As he cantered by I noticed he had knee-length boots and light-ish riding nether garments, and was wearing a mask. With a curious thrill, I realised he was a highwayman. He pulled up at a clump of trees a little further along, and backed his horse into the shadows. I felt terrified and daren't move.

A few minutes later came the sound of a horse-drawn carriage, and into view came a small coach pulled by two horses. The driver in a three-cornered hat sat on a high seat at the front of the coach. As the coach neared the trees, the highwayman cantered into the roadway, brandishing a long horse pistol, and called out in ringing tones. "Stand and deliver!"

The driver of the coach pulled up with a curse, and the highwayman ordered him to dismount and stand with his hands up. Then he rode to the coach door, doffed his hat, and said, "I beg of you to alight". At the same time opening the door and helping two terrified ladies to step down.

"Good evening", he said. "I regret I must trouble you to hand over your jewellery, but if you do this you will come to no harm".

Just then, the driver of the coach made a movement, and quick as a flash, the highwayman turned to him.

"Egad, sir, I've a mind to blow your brains out and will do if you don't stand still!".

While he was addressing the coachman, I noticed one of the ladies pull off a ring from one of her fingers and drop it at the roots of a tree against which she was standing. The highwayman now turned round and said, "Come, ladies, do as I ask quickly, for I have other work tonight". The lady who had thrown away her ring handed him a silver watch, whereupon the highwayman said, "Haven't you any rings?" "I have no rings", replied the lady. "Ah, you are a maiden then", said the highwayman, and courteously raised her hand to his lips. The other lady handed over a ring, a brooch and a watch. This was too much for me. I sprang from my hiding place and shouted, "You wretch. Give the ladies back their jewellery!". The highwayman turned round and fired his pistol.

I awakened, bathed in perspiration. It was some seconds before I realised I had been dreaming. Everything seemed so real. Eventually I dozed off again.

In the morning, the dream remained so vivid that I walked back to the road where I had found myself last night. Yes, there was the bush that I had stood behind, and there was the clump of trees behind which the highway- man had concealed himself. And opposite was the tree where one of the ladies had dropped her ring. I searched but of course found nothing. All that day I had the feeling that it really had happened, so at the weekend, I went back to the tree with a small trowel. I scraped away the dead leaves and dug among the roots, carefully sifting the soil. Apart from bits of flint and stones, there was nothing, and after half an hour I decided to give up. What was I expecting to find? It was only a dream after all. And then I saw it. A dirty, blackened ring. My heart thumped violently as I scraped the soil off it, but it was in such poor condition that I could make nothing of it. So I took it home, washed it in soap and water, and cleaned it. It was a silver ring, and on the inside was engraved, "To E.S. from G.S. 21st May 1739".

P. J. Barsby

THE ADVENTURES OF LITTLE JOHN AND THE OUTLAWS OF SHERWOOD FOREST

Synopsis

When Robin Hood died, the King ordered the Sheriff of Nottingham to get rid of the band of outlaws in Sherwood Forest forthwith, under penalty of losing his office as Sheriff. But under the leadership of Little John, the outlaws put up a stiff resistance, and their exciting adventures are told in this original new story.

It tells of the infiltration into the band by one of the Sheriff's men and the resultant kidnapping of the son of Alan-a-Dale; the demand by the Sheriff; the rescue attempt; the outlaws revenge; the Goose Fair incident; the Militia attack; the flight into Barnsdale Forest; the meeting with Blackbeard and his outlaw band; adventures in Barnsdale; Little John saves the life of Blackbeard; the return to Sherwood; the problems of Sir Brian Maltravers; the discomforture of the Abbots; the expulsion of two thieves in the camp and the tragic consequences; Letitia of Lenton and her predicament; the Mansfield widow's appeal and the consequences; the capture of Little John by the Sheriff; the fight in Nottingham; and the last desperate stand in Sherwood Forest against the King's Militia, when many of Little John's band were killed. The King's officers were so impressed with the courage and bravery of the outlaws in the last desperate battle that they recommended the King's Pardon. Some of the band entered into the King's service, and others returned to their homes to live in peace.

Little John returned to his cottage in Hathersage, Derbyshire, where he lived for many years. When he died, he was buried in the churchyard, and his cap and bow hung in Hathersage Church, where they remained for many years. His grave is still to be seen in the churchyard, protected by iron railings. Thus ends this story of the outlaws of Sherwood Forest, an epic period in the history of England, the like of which we shall never see again.

Many of the places in Nottingham and the county associated with Robin Hood and his band are still in existence and are woven into the story.

THE BRANSTONS

A family saga.

CHARACTERS

THE FATHER. Adolphus Branston. A recently retired University professor. Sports a goatee beard and has a dry sense of humour. Can never remember where he has put his spectacles. Has been known to be looking all over for them when he has got them on. When his attention was drawn to this, he replied, "Well you can see better what you are looking for with your spectacles on". He has a rapport with animals and is fond of babies when they are quiet. His hobbies are writing, painting and bird watching.

THE MOTHER. Helen Branston. A retired office worker, ten years younger than her husband. Has a placid nature and acts as peacemaker in the household when required. Her hobbies are knitting garments for the grandchildren while watching television, and gardening in the summer.

THE SON, Reginald Branston is in his mid- thirties, unmarried and lives at home. He is a bit of a know-it-all whose bright ideas don't always work out, but he is always willing to help and offer advice. He has had several girl friends but the romances do not seem to last. He is very fond of the family cat and loves all animals. His hobby is photography, and taking long walks by himself.

TWO MARRIED DAUGHTERS, Alice and Joan and their husbands, who are responsible between them for the six grandchildren, live close by and are frequent visitors to the parental home.

SYNOPSIS

Each episode should contain some humour provided mainly by Reginald, but the forgetfulness of the professor can also have a place. Other members of the family, e.g. the two beautiful daughters, can be introduced frequently, depending on the story line. Each episode could contain a complete story, but when all the characters have been introduced, it may be well to consider a story with a problem for one of the characters which would require two or three episodes to resolve.

SAMPLE EPISODE

The episode could open with Mrs. Branston in the garden, setting plants which she has bought from the market. Reginald goes up to her and suggests that they should buy a greenhouse and grow their own plants which would be cheaper than buying them from the market.

She agrees, and the next shot shows Reginald on the way to the local garden centre to order one. A few days later a greenhouse arrives in a neat package with full instructions for its erection.

Reginald spends some time studying the instructions. He lays the separate pieces on the ground as instructed, but is not sure which piece goes where and tries several positions. In stepping back he puts his foot through what was one of the windows. He fetches the professor to help. They try different pieces and eventually agree.

There is just enough room for the greenhouse to stand between the garage and the path. After a tremendous struggle they get the greenhouse up.

Proudly they fetch Mrs. Branston to admire their handiwork. She looks all round and finally asks "How do I get in? You've got the door on the wrong side".

At that moment there is a toot on a motor horn, and the two married daughters, Alice and Joan and their husbands arrive. They are going into town and wondered whether Mrs. Branston wanted anything.

It was explained to them about the greenhouse door being on the wrong side, and with the four men taking a corner each of the greenhouse, they manage to lift it and turn it round.

And they take the measurement of the broken window and agree to call in at the glaziers and get a piece of glass cut to the required size.

And Reginald says he will have no difficulty in fixing it.

END OF EPISODE

SAMPLE EPISODE

The episode could open with Mrs. Branston in the garden setting plants which she has bought from the market. Reginald goes up to her and suggests that they buy a greenhouse and grow their own plants which would be cheaper than buying them from the market. She agrees, and the next shot shows Reginald on the way to the local garden centre to order one. A few days later a greenhouse arrives in a neat package with full instructions for its erection. Reginald spends some time reading the instructions. He lays the separate pieces on the ground as instructed but is not sure which piece goes where and tries several positions.

In stepping back he puts his foot through what was one of the windows.

He fetches the professor to help. They try different pieces and eventually agree. There is just enough room for the greenhouse to stand between the garage and the path. After a tremendous struggle they get the greenhouse up. Proudly they fetch Mrs. Branston to admire their handiwork. She looks all round and finally asks "How do I get in? You've got the door on the wrong side".

At that moment there is a toot on a motor horn , and the two married daughters, Alice and Joan, with their husbands arrive. They are going into town and wondered whether Mrs. Branston wanted anything.

It was explained to them about the greenhouse door on the wrong side, and with the four men taking a corner each of the greenhouse, they manage to lift it and turn it round. And they take the measurements of the broken window and agree to call at the glaziers and get a piece of glass cut to the required size.

And Reginald says he will have no difficulty in fixing it.

THE COTTAGE GHOST

In the winter of 1843, the tenants of a lonely cottage in the Midlands were mystified by a persistent knocking on the window frame. The sounds were described as "like a swede turnip being bashed against the window".

Night after night the assault continued. Glass was shaken from the leaded window, but no missile could be found, nor were footsteps heard. The tenants reported the matter to the landlord, who decided to try to solve the mystery himself.

Accordingly he made a frame of brown paper coated with oil and lamp black; and after dark removed the shutters and substituted the paper frame. At a few yards, it was impossible to notice the alteration.

That night, the landlord and his brother stationed themselves in the cottage after dark, unknown to anyone but the tenants. They took the precaution to sit well clear of the window in case a missile came through the brown paper. They had not long to wait.

Suddenly there came a thunderous knocking, the windows rattled. but nothing came inside. They dashed out, but there was no sign of anyone, nor was there a mark on the coated paper.

Then a score of hefty young men from the village decided to keep watch. Late at night they concealed themselves inside and outside the cottage and waited. An hour passed by. Nothing happened. Then, as midnight chimed the hour from a distant clock, there came a sudden knocking on the window frame. The waiting men in the cottage dashed out and joined those outside. They had not seen anything, not even a ghostly figure. And the knockings had ceased.

By now, the fame of the cottage ghost had spread far and wide, and special trains were run on Sundays to enable curious sightseers to gaze at the cottage. Disappointed at not seeing anything out of the ordinary they would repair to the two local inns and listen avidly to the tales told by the locals over a pint of beer. It is said that the publicans made a small fortune out of the affair and eventually retired.

At length the visitors became such a nuisance that the cottage was closed, and remained uninhabited for a long time.

Then one day, the villagers were amazed to find that the cottage had been let again. Speculation was rife as to how long the new tenant would stay before the ghost got on his nerves. He was an old man in poor circumstances, who had begged to be allowed to live in the cottage at a small rent. It was pointed out to him that the cottage was haunted. But he didn't mind, he wasn't afraid of ghosts.

A year later, a nervous wreck, the old man gave up the tenancy. He explained that while he didn't believe in ghosts, the constant knocking got on his nerves. Thereupon the owner closed the cottage, and it remained closed until after the first World War, when it was let during the housing shortage. But no more was heard of the ghost. What caused the knockings? It is known that at the time, a pedlar was in the habit of making a regular call in the village. Suddenly his visits ceased, and he was never seen again. This caused some surprise, as some of the villagers had ordered goods from him. His last known call was to the isolated cottage at which the subsequent knockings occurred.

The lane to the cottage was very muddy, and he had asked a farmer who lived nearby for permission to take a short cut through his orchard to the cottage where he intended to stay the night, as the tenants were friends of his. The farmer readily gave him permission, and that was the last anyone saw of the pedlar. Except for the tenants of the cottage.

About that time, a former parish constable living in a cottage about a mile away had a horrible dream. He dreamed that a man was being murdered in an orchard by a person brandishing an axe. His own cottage had an orchard attached, and the dream was so vivid it awakened him. He got up and walked round the orchard but found nothing untoward.

Returning to bed, he lay tossing about, unable to sleep. Then he remembered that a cottage over the hill was set in an orchard, so he got up again and walked over the hill to this cottage. He was somewhat surprised to see two men digging in the garden by the light of a lantern. It was about 5 o'clock in the morning.

Approaching the two men, whom he recognised as the tenant of the cottage and his son, he enquired what they were doing in the garden at such an early hour. The older man, who seemed rather flustered, said he had got up early to make an onion bed, his wife having risen early to do the washing. Sounds of scrubbing could plainly be heard coming from the kitchen and this seemed to support his explanation.

Apart from his dream, the former parish constable had no grounds for disbelieving the man and after a few more words he returned home.

The next morning, the vividness of his dream had considerably dimmed and he came to the conclusion that it was just a coincidence that he should find two men digging in the garden. He knew that both men worked long hours at an ironworks a few miles away, and it seemed a feasible explanation that they had got up early to do some gardening at daybreak before they went to work, as it would be too dark in the evening when they returned home. So he came to the conclusion that his suspicions the night before were unfounded and were probably the result of his strange dream.

Some months later, when the two men were assisting the local farmer with the harvest, there was a scene between the tenant of the cottage and his wife, who had come to the harvest field to bring his tea.

An argument developed, and he threatened to kick her off the field if didn't stop nagging, whereupon she shouted, "You daren't. I could hang you any day. I have your coat of arms in the bedroom". There was an uneasy silence until she had gone, followed by her husband and son, then the others discussed what she could have meant by her strange words. They felt sure it related to the missing pedlar.

Suspicion increased when it became known that the tenant's daughter was giving away print stuff which she said an aunt had sent her.

None of the villagers could recall the family mentioning an aunt before, and in any case, why should an aunt send her material to give away? They were a poor family and had never been known to give anything away. A rumour got round that it was part of the pedlar's stock, and as the rumour spread, the family suddenly left the district.

Soon afterwards, the woman died, and in her last illness, it was said that the husband would never allow her to be alone when the doctor or the parson called. After his mother's death, the son married and left home, and sometime afterwards the after married again. His second wife was said to have had an uneasy time. Her husband turned morose, with fits of violence. Eventually he became ill, and as he lay dying, his wife fled to the nearest cottage a quarter of a mile away and told the neighbour she could stand it no longer.

Night after night, she said, her husband sat up in bed, and pointing to a corner of the room, cried out "There he is. I murdered him and buried the axe in the brook".

The neighbour returned with the terrified wife, and found the man had died. The knockings at the cottage ceased at that time. Years afterwards an axe was found in the brook but the body of the pedlar was never found. The villagers firmly believed that the knockings were caused by a disembodied spirit endeavouring to call attention to the crime, and when the murderer died, the spirit was at rest.

One thing is certain. There will be no more knockings. The cottage was demolished to make way for a housing estate.

THE HAUNTED GYPSY

Editor's note: "Gorgio" is the Gypsy word for a "non-gypsy", "matto" is drunk, "chavi" is a young girl, "chavo" is a young boy, "gavver" is a policeman, "dickler" is a sheet.

The Romani vans farthest from the fire showed up ghostly in the evening mist, which rose from the damp grass to half way up the wagon wheels. But the fire was warm and cheerful as we sat around on a late autumn evening. It was Halloween, and somehow the talk turned to witches and ghosts.

Old Josiah, the boss of the camp, was a born story teller, and the talk seemed to revive memories. Rolling a cigarette, he lit it with a brand from the fire, took one or two satisfying puffs, then began. "About seventy years ago, when I was a young chavo, one of our men named Jake had a row with his missus 'cause she nagged him when he got drunk. She was always nagging him, like. This night, he came home matto, and they had a rare set to. They went at it hammer and tongs, and we didn't interfere 'cause it was a family squabble and we don't take part unless we are asked. Well, she continued kicking and scratching him and pummelling him with her fists until he suddenly draws his knife from his belt and stabs her in the chest. She looked at him with a funny sort of look and screamed, 'You'll pay for this, Jake - I'll haunt you till you die!', then she gives a sort of gurgle and drops down dead."

Her sister, who never liked Jake, shouted "You murderer! I'll fetch the gavvers to you!". And off she went to find the policeman who lived in the village nearby. While she was gone, Jake gathered a few things together and made off. It was about half an hour before Meg came back with the gavver, and by that time Jake was well away. The gavver asked us what had happened, and we told them we had heard them quarreling but hadn't seen what had happened 'cause it was dark. He went off and fetched a doctor who said she was dead, and later the Black Maria came and took her away.

In the morning, the gavvers came with a great bloodhound and asked for something Jake had worn. Meg gave him an old dickler belonging to Jake, which the dog sniffed, and off they went. They caught Jake hiding in a wood about three miles away, and took him to gaol. Well, there was a big trial and a lot of us had to go to court. Jake said as how he had only brought his knife out to frighten her and she had slipped when they were struggling and fell on the knife, and that's how she died. The gavvers asked us if we had seen what had happened, but we all said it was dark and we didn't see him stab her though we heard them quarreling. You see, we didn't want to make it worse for Jake. Well, the gavvers weren't sure that Jake really meant to kill her so they said it was manslaughter and Jake was put in prison.

In them days, we moved about a lot, going to different parts of the country, but we allus stopped at the same places each year. Well, it was about ten years later we were staying in the same spot where Jake had killed his missus, but we hadn't heard anything of him since. Then my Uncle came to stay with us and we got talking about old times and he told us what had happened.

Jake was let out of prison a year early because he hadn't caused any trouble, but he was told if he got into trouble again he would go back into gaol. He was scared that the police would be watching him all the time, so he daren't go out much in the daytime at first. But after a while he got over his fear of the gavvers and started calling at houses again. One day he went out begging at a big house that stood on its own.

A young maid opened the door, and though she was a gorgio, she was so pretty that Jake took a fancy to her. Jake was very handsome himself and he called the next day and got talking to her and persuaded her to visit the camp. Well, the upshot of it was he asked her to come and live with us, which she did. They didn't get married but lived together and of course he never told her about his first wife.

This girl from the big house soon became as much like a Romani as if she had allus lived in a van. She went out selling pegs and telling fortunes and looked after Jake like she was his wife. But after a while Jake turned a bit funny. He told us his dead wife seemed to be following him everywhere. Sometime he would wake up in the night screaming that his wife (the one he had murdered) was chasing him with a knife.

Uncle was in the next van and said that some nights it was terrible to hear him screaming. His second missus, the one he got from the big house, couldn't stand it any longer and left him. One night after she had gone, Jake asks my Uncle to go with him to the osier beds to cut sticks for making baskets. He didn't want to go because it was dark and he was frightened of Jake. But he thought he had better go or he might turn nasty. On the way, Jake told him he felt that he was always being watched, and he thought it might be the gavvers wanting to take him to prison. But he said he would never go back to gaol and he would fight anyone who tried to take him. They got to the osier beds and had cut a few sticks when Jake suddenly screams. "Look! There's my dead wife following me with a knife in her hand! My uncle looks round but he couldn't see anybody, so he says to Jake, "There's nobody following you - it's your guilty conscience for killing your wife".

Jake stares at him and says, "You shouldn't have said that. You're going to pay for that", and he whips out his knife. My Uncle was frightened and ran off, with Jake chasing him. Then Jake tripped up and fell, and my Uncle got away. He was scared to death and ran all the way back to camp. He told his wife what had happened and the kept the van door bolted all night. In the morning Jake had calmed down, but he had gone funny in the head and swore his dead wife was following him everywhere he went. And then, about a week later, in the middle of the night, there came a horrible scream from Jake's van. They all rushed to his van, and there he lay at the bottom of the van steps, with a knife in his chest. It may have been my imagination, but the night air suddenly seemed to go chilly, and the mist swirled like a creeping ghost. I was glad of the warmth of the fire.

Old Josiah paused to roll another cigarette before continuing. "They never did find out who done it", he said slowly. Y'see, the knife what was sticking in his chest wasn't his own knife. It belonged to his dead wife".

THE MIRROR

Browsing round a local car boot sale, I picked up a small mirror, mounted in a green plastic frame. It was about 3 inches by 2 inches, ideal for slipping in my pocket for the odd occasions when I needed a mirror. It was only 10p, so I bought it.

When I got home I had another look at it, and was intrigued to read on the back in a childish hand, Alice, her mirror. Who was Alice? Obviously a child from the handwriting. And how had it come to be on a stall at a car boot sale?

As I gazed into the mirror, ruminating on the questions raised by the writing on the back, my face seemed to disappear from the glass and was replaced by that of a child about eight years old, with blue eyes and flaxen curls. She was smiling, and appeared to be looking straight at me. It was a few seconds before I realised I had been day-dreaming, but the impression of a smiling child was quite vivid. She must have been fond of the mirror to put her name on the back of it, so why had she parted with it? Perhaps she had lost it, or might have had it stolen at school.

The more I thought about it, the more I became intrigued. Perhaps she was even now bemoaning the loss of her favourite mirror. I felt I ought to do something to try to find her and restore it to her

Eventually, I decided to put a small advertisement in the local free paper which circulated in a wide area. "ALICE. I have your mirror. Telephone 254942 if you would like it back".

About three weeks later I had a telephone call. Picking up the handset, I quoted the number, and a woman's voice asked," Are you the person who put an advertisement in the Recorder about Alice's mirror?"

P. J. Barsby

"That's right", I replied.

"Well, I'm Alice's mother. She lost the mirror when we were on holiday in Mablethorpe. She was very much upset, as she called it her looking- glass and said she could see faces in it, and used to talk to them. She's only eight. I bought her another mirror but she didn't like it. She's at present in hospital recovering from meningitis, and I wondered if you would let me have the mirror to take to her. I'm sure it would help in her recovery, as she was so attached to it".

"Of course I will. Where do you live?" I jotted down the address, which was in Sheffield. "I'll put it in the post today".

"It's very kind of you, sir. I'll pay you for your trouble".

"Not at all. I'm only too pleased to let her have it. And I hope she will soon be better".

I wrapped the mirror between two pieces of stout cardboard and sent it by recorded delivery, with a little note. "Here is your mirror, Alice. Hope you will, soon be better".

About a week later, I had a letter, thanking me for my trouble, and enclosing a letter from Alice. Written in capital letters, it read

> THANK YOU FOR SENDING MY LOOKING GLASS. WHEN I LOOKED INTO IT I SAW YOUR FACE. YOU ARE A KIND MAN WITH A MOUSTACHE LIKE MY DADDY HAD. I LIKE YOU.
>
> LOVE,
>
> ALICE

I was very touched by the letter and its obvious sincerity, and somewhat puzzled how she knew that I had a moustache.

A month later, I was surprised to receive a letter with a Sheffield post-mark. Opening the flap, I drew out a single folded sheet, which read:

```
Dear Mr. Dixon,

I am glad to say that Alice has made a
complete recovery and is now back home.
She is continuously asking to see "that
nice man who sent me my looking-glass".

I wonder whether it is possible to arrange
a meeting.  I don't have a car but could
come by train on a day to suit yourself.
But if you would rather visit us at home,
you would be most welcome.  I do hope we
can arrange a meeting, as Alice is so
persistent and I am sure it would help to
continue her recovery.  In any case, I
would like to thank you again for your
kindness in returning the mirror.

Yours sincerely,


Joyce Lee
```

I was at first very undecided what to do. The idea of asking them to come by train, with all the difficulties of travel, not to mention the expense, seemed rather ungallant, added to which my bachelor flat was not very presentable. It would only take me about an hour in the car to visit them at home, and the prospect of seeing whether my "vision" when looking in the mirror, of a flaxen haired girl with blue eyes was a reality, intrigued me. So I decided to go, and phoned Mrs. Lee with suggested dates. She seemed overjoyed and we fixed up a date and time to suit us both.

When I arrived at the house, with its neatly bordered front lawn, I rang the bell and an attractive woman of about thirty five opened the door. I introduced myself, and her face lit up with pleasure as she invited me in. A young girl with flaxen curls and blue eyes came running up, and said, "I'm Alice. You're just as nice as I knew you'd be", and flung her arms round me. It was rather embarrassing but very pleasing.

It was easy to see where the child got her good looks from. Mrs. Lee had the same flaxen hair and blue eyes, and was indeed a very attractive woman.

While she got the tea ready, I wondered where the husband was. Was he still at work, or was she divorced?

As though in answer to my thoughts, she said, as she poured out the tea, "My husband died two years ago of cancer. He had an operation but it was too late. I nursed him for two years before he died. He was only thirty-six when he died". There was no sign of self pity in her voice, just a matter of fact statement. I noticed the little lines of suffering round the corners of her mouth as she spoke, which gave character to her still beautiful face. She paused, then said, "But I mustn't keep talking about myself. What about you. Are you married?"

"No", I replied. "I'm just a confirmed bachelor. At least, I thought I was, until now" I added after a pause. She looked into my eyes and we both smiled. And it was then that I knew that I loved her. We've been married now six months, and I can honestly say they have been the happiest six months of my life.

And all because of 10p spent on a little mirror at a car boot sale.

Articles

These are the various articles that were found on the computer disks.

AN ABSORBING HOBBY

My hobby has all the excitement of the hunter; the thrill of the explorer; the fascination of the collector; and the satisfaction of possessing interesting objects. In short, I am an avid collector, and have built up my own home museum.

I started out by collecting fossils, knapped flints, arrow heads, Roman coins, pottery and the like. This is a relatively inexpensive form of collecting. A search along a river bank, gravel pit, or a ploughed field, or even your own garden, may reveal pieces of flaked or knapped flint, unusual stones, and fragments of pottery. So the next time you take a walk in the countryside, keep your eyes open for 'finds'. It will greatly add to the interest of the walk.

Photograph No.1 shows several objects I have collected in this manner, including flint arrow heads, scrapers, celts (stone hammers), fossils, and Roman pottery. One interesting stone has a hole through the centre.

It is essential when you start collecting to keep a record of the date of the find, where found, and a brief description of the object. A piece of gummed envelope flap will do, though one can buy adhesive tape quite cheaply, and this is ideal for the purpose. A shirt box makes a cheap and handy container for such a collection, the objects being sellotaped to the bottom of the box, or on to a separate piece of card to fit the bottom of the box.

My other collections are of native craftwork and unusual objects.

Photograph No.2 shows a fossil; part of a head carving from Peru; an African bone necklace; a fossilised underwater plant from Jamaica; an Eskimo soapstone carving; a North American Indian arrow head from Montana; an ivory cigarette holder from India; a gypsy peg; an Indian ornament; and a hardwood knife from Peru.

If you are unable to travel and wish to make a collection of items from abroad, write to the editors of newspapers in the area in which you are interested, telling them of your hobby and asking for pen friends who would be willing to exchange articles. This in itself can be another rewarding spin-off from the hobby of collecting. You can obtain the addresses of foreign newspapers by perusing the Press Guides (Willings and others) in your local public library.

Photograph No.3 is from my collection of North American Indian craftwork, including an elk skin quiver for arrows; a pair of moccasins; a beaded headband; a medicine man's 'charm'; a bone scraper and an eagle wing whistle.

Collecting can be a fascinating hobby, relatively inexpensive and one which increases one's knowledge of other countries, places, and peoples.

P. J. Barsby

IS IT REALLY NECESSARY?

For pop groups to jig about as though they are bursting to go to the loo when they are performing.

For the person in front of you in the post office queue to be purchasing a month's supply of national insurance stamps when all you want is second class stamp.

For television audiences to indulge in frantic clapping at a mediocre performance.

For visitors who have "not come to stay" to remain so long.

For everyone at the hotel to come trying the bathroom door just after you have sneaked in.

For pop singers to appear to be in agony when they are singing.

For pedestrians to dilly-dally at the edge of the pavement until a car comes along and then dash forward and backward on a pedestrian crossing.

For neighbours to slam car doors at one o'clock in the morning.

For the bad guy in Westerns to squint his eyes and talk out of the side of his mouth.

For courting couples to assume that that their partners are unable to walk unaided.

For hostesses to mumble when they introduce one to perfect

strangers.

For the dog to muddy your step just after you have cleaned it.

For the bus to be on time when you are a few seconds late.

For the milk to boil over the minute you stop watching it.

For after-dinner speakers to be "reminded of a story" when they have been rehearsing it for weeks.

For friends to drop in when you are watching your favourite programme on television.

For so many people to be ambling aimlessly on the pavement when you are dashing to catch a train.

For the bus conductor to give you so much small change when you tender a pound coin.

For the milkman to make such a clatter when he delivers the milk at six o'clock in the morning.

For the person sitting in front of you at the theatre to waggle about so much.

For anyone to be the life and soul of the party.

For cereal packets to be so tall and thin that they are easily knocked over.

For doctors to write out prescriptions so illegibly.

For income tax to be paid by old age pensioners.

For menus to be printed in French.

To continue our illogical system of spelling.

To keep up with the Jones's.

To have all the petty-fogging restrictions with which we are inflicted.

To travel at seventy miles an hour on any road.

To make derogatory remarks about a person we don't like.

To teach sex to children in primary schools.

To waste time and paper beginning letters with "Dear sir", and ending with "Yours faithfully" or worse, "I am, sir, your obedient servant".

To give tips to people who are paid for their services.

To import so many trashy American programmes for our television.

To have party-political broadcasts.

To publish so much ballyhoo about show people.

To pay death duties on money which has already been the subject of income tax.

To sever links with the past by pulling down fine old property to make way for modern "development".

To grumble at our weather, which is the most varied in the world.

To put up with litter louts, vandals, poor service and rudeness.

Well, is it necessary? Or can we do something about it?

P. J. Barsby

LUCKY YOU

"Some people are born lucky!". How often do we hear this phrase? And there seems to be some truth in it - we all know people who seem to have more than their fair share of luck, while others seem most unlucky.

But don't worry if you consider yourself to be in the latter category. The "experts" tell us there are many ways of attracting to ourselves the mysterious quality known as luck. One of the methods most frequently advocated is the wearing or carrying of some "charm" or talisman. Brooches or pendants in the form of miniature horseshoes, four-leaf clover, shamrock, pixies, gnomes, etc. are favourites in this respect, while the carrying of a rabbit's foot is considered to be very lucky. But it seems that the value of the charm lies in the amount of faith one places in it. If you really believe that something will bring you luck, you adopt an optimistic frame of mind and think "success" thoughts which attract the desired thing to you.

Each person is supposed to have a lucky number, corresponding to one's birth date, and the use of this number on occasions may bring you luck. For example, if you were born on the 14th February 1959, your lucky number is 4. (14+2+1+9+5+9=31 (3+1) = 4. So that if you purchase a raffle ticket, you will endeavour to get one that has a number of fours in it, or the total figures on which can be reduced to four.

Similarly, your lucky number can be used on the pools coupons. Select the teams against which the number in the column can be reduced to your lucky number. For example, if your lucky number is 3, select the teams whose numbers are 3, 12, 21, 30, 33, 39 and so on. You then stick to these numbers each week and hope for the best.

The wearing of your favourable colour is said to bring you luck. Thus, for those born in January (up to the 20th) the favourable colours are grey, violet, purple and black. From the 21st January to the 20th February, the colours are electric blues and greys; March - purple, mauve, violet; April - pink, rose, crimson; May - all shades of blue; June - silver and white; July - green, cream, white; August – yellow, gold, green, white, cream; September - silver grey; October - blue and violet; December - violet and mauve.

It is considered lucky to find and wear white heather, but it is unlucky to bring it into the house. Black cats are "lucky" and if one crosses your path you are in for a spot of luck. If the household cat sneezes in front of the fire, this is considered to be especially lucky. If you are unlucky at cards, try blowing through the pack while shuffling. This should change your luck. There seems to be no reason why it should, but just try it.

It is considered lucky to touch a sailor's collar, to see a piebald horse (but don't look at the tail), accidentally to wear something inside out, to find a horse shoe, or even a horse shoe nail, to carry or wear something made of iron, and to receive a gift of yellow flowers (money is on the way).

Some days are considered to be luckier than others. To find out which days of the month are lucky for you, add your "lucky number" to the day of the month on which you propose to do something special. If the resultant number adds up to 3, 5, 7, 10, 11, 17, 19, 20 or 21, these days are specially lucky for you. Days to avoid are those which add up to 8, 12, 13, 15, 16, and 18, which are

P. J. Barsby

not propitious. Whether you believe in luck or not, there is no doubt that, other things being equal, one per cent of luck often means the difference between success and failure.

So here's wishing you luck.

PRACTISING POETRY

Do you sometimes find it difficult to think of an idea for a poem?

Or having an idea, don't know whether to make it a rhyming poem or free verse?

While it is not possible to lay down hard and fast rules for writing poetry, which is such a personal affair, perhaps an outline of how I go about it might be of help.

First, the subject. This may be inspired by something I see or hear or 'feel' , or it may be the subject set for a competition, on which I have no preconceived ideas. In either case I write down everything that comes into my head concerning the subject. If rhyming words occur to me I jot them down, also any outstanding phrase. Sometimes a single phrase may set the 'mood' or even the meter. A couple of examples may help.

The subject set for a competition was Hunger. My mind went back to the time I spent in India where there was a great deal of abject poverty. So I wrote down: Beggars asking for "Baksheesh". Skinny woman with baby at breast, moaning incessantly. The death rate through malnutrition while food was wasted in other parts of the world. Vultures that hovered above carcasses. The distended stomach and staring eyes of hungry children. The gratitude in the eyes of a woman with a child to whom I gave a few annas. The continual cry of "Baksheesh, sah'b, baksheesh!" It occurred to me that this cry could be made the last line of verses. and the woman's thanks, "Mirhbani", could be included. Indian women carry their babies in a shawl on their backs or sitting astride their hips.

Staring eyes' and 'mother's thighs' suggested a rhyming couplet as did 'poorly dressed' and 'breast'. So it became a rhyming poem.

> Distended stomach, staring eyes
> He sits across his mother's thighs
> As she continuously cries
> "Baksheesh, sah'b, baksheesh!"
> Thin and haggard, poorly dressed
> Her baby suckling skinny breast
> She moans persistent, without rest
> "Baksheesh,m sah'b baksheesh".
> A rupee given, the attitude
> of despair ceases. Gratitude
> shines in her eyes. Her voice subdued
> "Mirhbani, sah'b, mirhbani!"
> In India's hot and dusty land
> The spectre of hunger, claw-like hand
> Beckons the vultures from the sand
> To witness human pain.
> And in the West, with napkins white
> In five-starred hotels subdued light
> They eat until their skins are tight
> While the hungry cry in vain.

On a visit to Newark in Nottinghamshire, I sat by the riverside, gazing at the ruins of the old castle, which had witnessed many stirring events during its long history. I visualised the castle in its heyday, when kings and queens and nobility assembled there for lavish entertainment. Now it was a ruin but kept from falling into total decay by the Ministry of the Environment. It seemed to me a noble ruin but a rather pathetic link with the past. Only the river was unchanged, and it had been flowing even before the castle was built. With these thoughts in mind, the following poem almost wrote itself.

> Window spaces, like sightless eye sockets
> in crumbling walls, stare across
> the flowing river.
> Grass grows in the great hall, where
> kings, princes, high born ladies
> danced and flirted.
> These ancient walls, preserved by modern skill
> stand proud, yet forlorn, like an old man,
> living beyond his time;
> pondering the years long gone,
> never to return;
> and the river, rimeless as eternity,
> flows on.

Although most modern poems do not rhyme, they do have a certain form. One way of achieving this is by a syllable count. Let us examine the following poem, which appears simple.

> I glanced up
> as he gave her
> a fond salute
> on the lips.
> And I saw
> for a moment
> the plain face
> glow with beauty.

The syllable count is 3-4-4-3 3-4-4-3 which gives it form. When you have completed a poem, put it aside for a few days. Then read it again. You will probably find that some alteration will make an improvement. Don't be satisfied with your first draft unless, after re-reading it some days later, you feel it cannot be bettered. Writing poetry is not easy, but if you make a practice of setting down your thoughts as they occur, then assembling them into some 'shape' quite often the final form of the poem will seem to suggest itself.

PUBLISH YOUR OWN WORK

To sum up:

Be critical in selecting material.

Decide on size of book and number of pages.

Decide on print run and obtain quotations.

Accept quotation and prepare dummy for printers

Check proofs and decide on selling price.

Decide on a suitable occasion for launching.

Obtain publicity in the local press and the little presses.

Write your own small posters and exhibit in local shops.

Display copies of the book at local functions

Sell copies to local libraries, shops, and booksellers.

Give talks to local groups and sell copies afterwards.

I would emphasis this is merely my own method of working. I don't claim that it is the best method, or the only method of working, but it has been successful with me and may well be successful with you.

So don't be put off by the initial cost of publishing your own work.

By good publicity and selling techniques, you can make a satisfactory profit, even though it may take a year or more. In my own case, I have succeeded in making a profit within six months of publication.

THEN AND NOW PHOTOGRAPHS

Today, nostalgia is big business, and the astute photographer can share in the profits.

Look through your old photograph albums and select any local views that have changed during the years. These may include buildings since demolished, country lanes widened, trees felled, and land now built on.

Now take new photographs from the same position as the old ones, and send them in 'pairs' to your local newspapers and to the county magazine as a "Then and Now" feature. The two illustrations have sold many times

Going through my old albums, I came across so many views that had altered that I decided to publish them as a booklet. I had kept all the negatives and had them printed. Then I took new photographs from the same positions and put two on a page, with the new one first, giving the date, and the old one underneath with the date. A local firm of printers printed the book, which I published myself and made a tidy profit.

If you hear of any likely alterations in your area, take shots immediately in black and white and colour. You will be acquiring a collection which will increase in value and profitability as the years go by. And when you have sufficient "Then and Now" photographs, consider publishing them as a booklet and selling locally. It can be very profitable.

Personal Memories

This is a collection of personal memories.

SHOECAPS

During the Great War, all soldiers had to wear puttees as an essential part of their uniform. These consisted of long strips of khaki cloth which was wrapped round the legs, beginning at the ankles and finishing below the knees, where they were tied with tape. They were worn to support the legs during the long marches the troops had to. In the case of the cavalry regiments, the wrapping was started just below the knees finishing at the ankles. This was to prevent the puttees from riding up when mounting the horses, and to accommodate the spurs.

A friend of the family when home on leave left a pair of puttees at our house. My brother and I persuaded mother to cut them in half to provide us with a set each which we proudly wore to school.

When the annual school medical examination came along, the medical officer asked us why we were wearing them. We said "to look like soldiers". He consulted the headmaster, who said that we walked four miles each day to and from school and could see no harm being done. The medical officer told us we could continue wearing them to school provided we took them off when we got home and didn't wear them all the time. We continued to wear them to school and were the envy of the other boys, who had to be content to wear military badges We noticed that soldiers boots didn't have toecaps, so we persuaded mother when buying the next pair of new boots (we didn't wear shoes in those days) to have them without toecaps as we claimed they were more comfortable to wear.

To raise money for comforts for the troops, the teacher would write on the blackboard "We will all bring a penny for our soldiers and sailors". We then had to copy this and take it to our parents.

When the penny (or more) was brought to school, we were awarded with a highly coloured certificate with our names on. This took place two or three times a year, notably on Empire Day and I think St George's Day.

COUNTRY SCHOOL

It was a mile to walk to the country school. We could either walk along the lane or go over the fields. One advantage of walking along the lane was that we could occasionally get a surreptitious ride behind a horse and cart, until the driver wondered why the cart suddenly tipped up with the weight of two or three boys hanging on the back; whereupon he would creep through the van and poke us off with his whip.

Another advantage of walking along the lane was that we could play cards on the way. Collecting cigarette cards was more than a pastime - it was a status symbol to own many cards, and gambling was one method of increasing one's stock. The game we played on the way to school was "Skims the Furthest" in which as we walked along we skimmed cards; and the one whose card landed the furthest away collected the other cards. of course, this slowed down our pace to school and meant us having to run the last half mile to get there before the bell stopped and the 'lines' were formed.

Going to school over the fields when the weather was fine was more attractive. We might find a golf ball on the golf links, or a bird's nest in the hedges. And we devised a simple system of getting a half day off from school. There was a brook running alongside a hedge, with a convenient large stone for standing on to look for minnows. We would encourage the youngest boy to stand on the stone, then give him a gentle nudge so that he overbalanced and fell into the brook. Then we quickly dragged him out, and one of us would take him home while the others would go on to school and explain to the headmaster that little Billy had fallen in the brook and Tommy had taken him home.

Of course, it only worked at very limited intervals, but one day we rescued a sheep that had got in the middle of the brook and was caught in the brambles. We all got wet this time, but were hailed as heroes when the story got out.

Other incidents come to mind - being caned for talking and inattention. A favourite trick was to hold out one's hand as directed, then when the cane came swishing down to smartly move the hand sideways so that the cane hit the master on the thigh. This was not appreciated by the master, and an extra vicious stroke followed.

Nature Study was always popular, as it usually meant going on a ramble over the golf links to measure the height of the old oak tree, see how many species of wild flowers we could name, or study the plant life and living creatures in the brook. I remember on one occasion seeing two frogs spawning and excitedly drawing the master's attention to "two frogs fighting each other". We were very innocent in those days.

Many of us had a collection of between 200 and 300 cigarette cards acquired mainly by gambling games, one of which was to aim cards at a wall in the playground. The first player to drop a card on those on the ground collected them all. One boy was a cripple in a wheelchair, who couldn't play this game, but he set up his own game consisting of a piece of board with six 'alleys' or entrances at the bottom of the board. The owner charged "three clean cards a go". Having paid the entrance fee you rolled up three marbles. If a marble rolled through an entrance, you collected the appropriate number of cards. More often than not, you lost.

The boy who ran this alley 'retired' with a fortune of more than 4,000 cigarette cards, which, as a noble gesture on his last day at school, he scattered in handfuls round the playground at playtime.

I can still remember the mad scramble that ensued to collect as many cards as possible before the bell rang. Yes, they were happy times at school.

NOTTINGHAM ZEPPELIN

There were seven of us in the house, my grandma and auntie,, our parents and we three children, my twin brother and I aged nine, and our younger brother aged seven. We didn't realise the danger we were in but it must have been a terrifying experience for the grownups whose anxiety communicated itself to us.

We didn't get much sleep that night, but the next morning, which was a Sunday, we joined the crowds to see the damage. A bomb had dropped on Woolworths in Wheeler Gate, but I don't recall any reports of looting. I found a fragment of the bomb, which had lodged in the tramlines, and have it to this day.

When we returned home, our neighbours told us they had heard the bombs, but had had a relatively peaceful night. Three years later there was to be a far bigger disaster in the area, which I shall recount in my next article.

P. J. Barsby

BOMB

It was a beautiful summer evening on July the first, 1918. My two
brothers and I were alone in our house in Elm Avenue, mother
having gone to the village post office to collect her allowance,
father being at the war. Suddenly at ten minutes past six, there was
the most ear splitting, paralysing bang I have ever heard, followed
by the sound of breaking glass as the windows of our house blew
in. We thought at first it was another Zeppelin raid, and promptly
dived into the cubby hole beneath the stairs, but after waiting a few
minutes and there being no more bangs, we came out. Looking
through the broken kitchen window, we saw a huge pall of
greenish black smoke drifting slowly towards us. In a few minutes
it descended on the village like a fog, blotting out the evening
sunlight as though there had been an eclipse. The sudden twilight
seemed eerie and menacing, and there was complete silence, as
though the world had come to an end.

Then we guessed what had happened. The national shell filling
factory about half a mile away had gone up. we had been warned
that in the event of an explosion, the fumes might be poisonous, so
we tied wet handkerchiefs round our noses and mouths and went
down the avenue to try to find mother. People were running down
Attenborough Lane from the direction of the factory, screaming
"Run for your lives, there's another hundred tons of TNT might go
up at any minute!"

Some ran down to the river, but having found mother in the fog,
we hurried up Long Lane with other villagers until we reached a
patch of greensward at the junction with Meadow Lane. Here we
felt we should be far enough away from the factory should there be
another explosion. My brothers and I went to the top of Meadow
Lane where it joins the main road and there we saw a tragic sight.

Horses and carts, drays, vans, lorries and cars were moving like a procession, taking the injured to Nottingham General Hospital.

When we returned home later that night, we could plainly see a gap in the factory where a building had stood, and a tall chimney had a gaping hole in its side, but was still standing. The village as covered in greyish green ash, looking like a long dead village with the dust of ages undisturbed.

134 employees were killed in the explosion, and many more injured.

Many were literally blown to bits and their remains are buried in a communal grave in Attenborough churchyard.

A COUNTRY SCHOOL DURING THE GREAT WAR

One incident in those far off days stands out in my memory above others. It was a beautiful summer evening on the 1st July 1918. My brothers and I were alone in the house, doing our homework. Mother had gone to the village post office to collect her allowances, father being at the War.

Suddenly the calm of the evening was shattered by the most ear splitting paralysing bang we had ever heard, followed by the sound of splintering glass as the windows of our house blew in.

We thought at first it was another Zeppelin raid, so we dived into the little cubbyhole under the stairs, waiting for the next bomb to fall. But there were no further bangs, so we came out and looked through the shattered window. A pall of greenish black smoke drifted slowly towards us, and descended on the village like a fog, blotting out the sunlight as though there had been an eclipse. The sudden twilight and the silence seemed eerie and menacing. Then we guessed what had happened. The shell filling factory about half a mile from the village had "gone up".

We had been warned that in the event of an explosion the fumes might be poisonous, so tying wet cloths round our noses and mouths, we went out to try to find mother in the fog. People were running down the lane from the factory shouting "Run for your lives. There's more tons of TNT may go up at any time!"

Eventually mother loomed up out of the fog, and along with other villagers we ran up the lane away from the factory until we reached a patch of greensward at the side of the lane far enough from the factory to be safe should there be another explosion. And there we rested.

My brothers and I walked to the top of the lane where it joined the main road, and there saw a tragic sight. Drays, vans and lorries were moving in a procession taking the injured to the hospital five miles away.

When we returned home later in the evening, we could see a gap in the factory where a building had been. A tall chimney was still standing with a gaping hole in its side. The village was covered in a greenish grey ash, looking as though it had been undisturbed for ages. We were relieved to find that our three weeks old pet rabbit was alive in his hutch, though covered in ash. One hundred and thirty four persons were killed in the explosion and are buried in a communal grave in our churchyard.

I was only 12 years old at the time, and shall never forget the terror of that fateful evening.

ATTENBOROUGH FOOTBALL CLUB

The club was originally formed in 1920 by my brother and I as the Attenborough Junior Football Club. We had a collection round the village which raised £2 towards the purchase of jerseys and shorts.

Our original strip was black and white striped jerseys and black shorts, but was later changed to blue shirts and white shorts.

Our home ground was a field on the other side of the brook from the village green, access to which was by a footbridge over the brook.

For several seasons we played friendly matches with some success, but in the 1926/7 season we entered Section B of the Long Eaton and District League. This was too strong for us, and it was suggested that we apply to the League for transfer to Section C, but at a special meeting of the club it was decided to remain in Section B even at the risk of losing every match. This was reported in the Football Post with a banner headline 'A Club with the will to stick to it' followed by an article captioned 'A Club with spirit'.

After 23 matches without a win, there appeared in the Football Post a long article with the byline "The Sports of Attenborough". Shortly afterwards, the impossible happened. We won our first match, beating Breaston Amateurs 2-1.

The Football Post came out with a banner headline across the centre pages, ATTENBOROUGH BOOK A WIN AT LAST, and the Derbyshire Football Express awarded us with a certificate for 'the most notable performance in the League'.

The next season was a better one, Attenborough causing a sensation by defeating the League leaders, Trent LMS 6-4,

Borrowash St Stephen's 5-1, and drawing 4-4 with British Celanese in the first round of the Beeston Cup, though we eventually finished bottom of the League, mainly due to seldom being able to field a full side.

The Club was disbanded at the end of the 1927/8 season, owing to the constant difficulty of raising a full team each week, and other factors. It was agreed to donate the £4 remaining in the kitty to the Derbyshire FA and the Notts FA Benevolent Funds.

Ten years later the club was revived by the curate, the Rev G. C. Spencer, under the title of Attenborough St Mary's Football Club. We again played in the Long Eaton and District League with some success, being runners-up in the 1940/1 season. Soon afterwards, war service put a stop to the activities of the club until after the war. My memories of the club in those far off days are of the reputation we gained for sportsmanship, and the rallying cry of "At'em Borough" when we were losing.

LOOSE WALLAH

"Sahib, Abdul is a loose wallah!"

I was lying on my charpoy outside the hut, and had just dozed off when I was wakened by a discreet cough, followed by this startling announcement. I sat up and gazed at the two chicos who stood before me. Umidard, the elder, who was making the accusation, was about twelve years old., and Abdul, the younger was nine and stood about two annas high. I shared the hut with my friend George and they were our bearers whose duty it was to wake us in the mornings if necessary, fill the lamps, clean the hut, keep things tidy, run errands, and generally make things easy for us.

"Me no loose wallah", protested Abdul with obvious sincerity and a worried expression on his baby face.

I tried hard to conceal a grin. A loose wallah in India is an evil man, a murderer or a robber, and a man to be avoided. The idea of little Abdul with the baby face being a loose wallah was distinctly funny.

"Now what have you been up to", I asked in magisterial tones. Before Abdul could reply, Umidard chipped in. "He smoke two of your cigarettes, sahib". "Has he, by Jove". I got up from the charpoy and went into the hut. to make sure. Yes, two cigarettes were missing from the packet. Not that I minded particularly, with the free issue we got, but petty thieving had to be put down at all costs. "Abdul", I said. "You've stolen two cigarettes, and I'm going to take you to the guard-room".

"Me no steal cigarettes, sahib. Umidard took them"

"Nay, sahib", protested Umidard. "Me saw Abdul take them".

I came to the conclusion that they had probably taken one each. But who had been the instigator of the theft? Umidard had made the accusation, but Abdul had strongly denied it. And I couldn't imagine little Abdul doing it unless persuaded by Umidard.

Listen", I said, "Two cigarettes are missing. If any more are missing, you both go to the guard-room jaldi. Thik hai?" (OK?) "Thik hai" they replied in chorus. "No more steal cigarettes."

Later in the afternoon, Abdul approached me. "Me no loose wallah", he began, and I agreed he wasn't. "Will you give me two annas off my pay, sahib?" "What do you want two annas for?" I asked. "Me no paisa, Me want two annas". "All right. But you know that if I give you two annas now, you will only get fourteen annas at the end of the week?". (A rupee was worth sixteen annas). "Thik hai, sahib". So I gave him two annas. And learned later that he had also borrowed three annas from George.

Back on the charpoy, I lay flat out in the shade of the verandah which ran the length of the hut. It was some comfort from the sweltering heat to lie undisturbed in the shade, clad only in a pair of shorts. I had lain for perhaps half an hour and was enjoying the peace of the afternoon when Umidard approached.

"Your cigarettes, sahib", he said, holding out a new packet.

"Where did you get these from?" I asked suspiciously.

"From the canteen, sahib."

"But I haven't ordered any. Take them back!"

"Nay sahib. They are for you. Abdul has sent them. Abdul pay for them. You no pay"

"But why", I asked. "Kiswaste?"

"Abdul smoke your cigarettes, so he buy you some more. No guard-room, sahib"

So that was why the little beggar had subbed two annas from me and three from George. The guard-room threat had evidently been effective. I swallowed a small lump that had come into my throat. "Thank Abdul for me. Tell him sahib says he no loose wallah. No guard-room". And off ran Umidard to convey the message.

At the end of the week, Abdul came for his pay. I was sitting on the charpoy with George. "Let me see", I said winking at George. "You borrowed two annas from me and three from George sahib. So if I give you fourteen annas and George sahib gives you thirteen, that will be right, won't it?" "Thik hai", he replied poker faced.

I looked at George and George looked at me. We both looked at Abdul's baby face and innocent expression. He was only nine years old. I handed him two rupees.

"That's from George sahib and me. You can keep the change", I said hurriedly as he fumbled in his pocket. Abdul's face lit up. "You good boss", he said. And then as an afterthought, with a smile on his face, "no guard-room!" It was worth the five annas to keep that cherubic smile on his face.

SALAAM

It happened during the war when I was stationed in Northern India.

Being off duty one afternoon, I decided to explore the vast plain on which we had an air strip. After walking about a mile, I came across a dried-up river bed and decided to follow its course.

About a mile further on I climbed up the right hand bank and was surprised to see, about three hundred yards away, an Indian village. It looked very beautiful, with the strong sunlight reflecting on the whitewashed, flat topped dwellings and the glittering white-domed mosque in the centre. I got out my sketchbook, and had just started to draw when an Indian maiden came down the footpath from the village, balancing two water jars on her head. She walked along gracefully until she reached the opposite bank, when she saw me, and immediately retraced her steps. Finishing my sketch, I got down into the river bed, intending to go on a little further.

It was then that I noticed an Indian watching me from the opposite bank. He was soon joined by another. Suddenly I realised that this must be the village which had been placed out of bounds to all service personnel after an airman had been savagely attacked and beaten up by the tribesmen.

The village headman had complained that the man had been spying on some of the women bathing naked in a pond near the village, and to keep the peace, our C.O. placed the village out of bounds.

I decided that the best thing was to retrace my steps and make my way back to camp as quickly as possible. The tribesmen were watching me, so I ostentatiously looked at my wristwatch, hesitated, then turned round and walked back the way I had come.

P. J. Barsby

After walking about a hundred yards, I noticed an Indian on the bank in front, peering at me from behind a small bush. Then he disappeared. By now I was getting rather alarmed. It looked as though they were closing in on me.

My worst fears were confirmed when on rounding a bend, I saw the Indian who had been on the bank had got down into the river bed and was approaching me. He had his right hand in his dhoti at waist level where these tribesmen carry a large curved knife. He slowly approached and I tried to walk nonchalantly towards him although I was scared stiff. Gradually the distance between us decreased and I wondered what was going to happen.

Then I had an inspiration. As he drew near I raised my right hand in salute and called out, "Salaam!" (a peace greeting). He seemed rather taken back and hastily withdrew his right hand and raised it, replying "Salaam, sahib!" and walked on past me.

I shall never know if my peace greeting forestalled any evil intentions, but I was very relieved to get safely back to camp.

A CHRISTMAS SERVICE IN INDIA

During the war, I was posted to India, where I spent two Christmases. By the time the second Christmas came round I was feeling homesick at the thought of my wife and children having to spend another Christmas without me. I felt the need to go to church as I would have done if I had been at home in England. It was already quite hot as I entered the little whitewashed church.

Beggars in tattered dirty garments sat outside, some of them maimed, and all piteously begging for baksheesh. Although a familiar sight in India, it seemed more poignant on this beautiful Christmas morning when one's thoughts turned to giving and receiving presents. The church was almost full but somehow room was found for me.

I was fortunate enough to be given a seat in the choir stalls. Others sat on hassocks or on the bare floor. Late comers said there was still a crowd outside who couldn't get in. Large fans were doing their best to keep the church cool, and the side door had been opened so that those outside could hear the service.

The congregation consisted mainly of Indian families; the women wearing beautiful coloured saris, the men in their best white dhotis. The children were like little replicas of their parents. There were a few white families and Anglo Indian families, and several Service personnel.

A space had been left in the centre for the Sunday School children, and in they came, bringing their presents for the poorer children. Near the pulpit was a huge Christmas tree which already had many presents hanging from the branches, including a large model aeroplane. Some of the children brought their presents wrapped in newspaper and tied with string, but they all brought something.

When the tree was lit up with coloured fairy lights, there was an audible gasp of delight from the children. They sang some primary hymns including "Away in a Manger" which touched me deeply, as it is one that my children sing at Sunday School, and they would probably be singing it in our church today. I noticed a little Indian girl in a sari sharing her hymn-book with a white girl and they were both smiling.

Then the Minister asked the children to bring their presents to the Christmas tree. It was very touching to see them bring their past treasures; books, toys and games for the poorer children who otherwise might not have had any presents.

We sang the well loved Christmas hymns, and the singing was very hearty. It was grand to hear one of the little girls singing away when everyone else had stopped. It was a happy service, very sincere and uplifting, and I came away feeling spiritually refreshed, and a little less homesick.

And now, when I hear the children singing "Away in a Manger" in our church, I sometimes think of that service in India all those years ago, and the uplift it gave me.

DEMOB

It was a Sunday afternoon in Delhi, and the sun's warm rays beat down from a cloudless sky. I was off duty and had come to the temple gardens to enjoy the serenity of the carefully tended flower beds, and the cool marble buildings with their exquisite patterns of inlaid semi- precious stones and their graceful archways.

The gardens were thronged with Indian families strolling leisurely to and fro, and I greatly admired the brightly coloured saris of the womenfolk, and their long sleek black hair which in many cases came down to below the waist. Their men folk were dressed more soberly in white, and there was quite a holiday atmosphere, with the ubiquitous cha wallahs, the sweet-meat sellers, and the cheapjacks doing a brisk trade.

Having made a tour of the temples and the gardens, I found a secluded spot where I could indulge in my favourite pastime of lying on my back on the grass, enjoying the sunshine and letting the world go by.

Some minutes later I was disturbed by a voice which seemed to come to me in my dreams. "Sahib, you have a lucky moustache!"

I opened my eyes and looked up. In front of me stood a smiling Sikh wearing a turban and spotlessly white dhoti and pantaloons. I wasn't quite sure whether the remark was addressed to me or not.

"Sahib" he repeated. "May I speak to you? I have something important to tell you".

I was a little bit annoyed at being wakened from my reverie, and rightly suspected he was a fortune teller. I had been pestered before by these gentlemen wanting to tell my fortune, and the opening gambit was familiar. You have a lucky moustache or a lucky face. So rather ungraciously I asked him what he wanted to tell me. "Please don't be angry at what I have to tell you, but there is someone dear to you who is ill. Her name begins with "M".

I was rather startled but tried not to show it. In my pocket was a letter from my wife Mabel, telling me she was suffering from a nervous upset. She had been ordered by the doctor to rest and had been in bed a fortnight but was now recovering. How could this Sikh possibly know of this?

He was speaking again. "Don't worry, sah'b. She is even now getting better. And there are other things I could tell you".

"All right", I said. "Tell me the date I shall be demobilised".

This was a leading question, as at that time no one knew when the war would end. By now, quite an interested crowd had gathered to listen to the conversation. Indians are intensely curious at anything that promises to give free entertainment.

"Come this way, sahib" said the Sikh. "There are too many people here". He led me to another part of the gardens where we could talk undisturbed by the passers by. We sat on the grass, and he produced a piece of paper. Writing something on it, he screwed it up and asked me to put it in my pocket. I did so. Then he asked me to think of a flower. I thought of a violet as being an unlikely flower to be found in India. He then produced another piece of paper on which were written several letters of the alphabet. "Point to the first letter of the flower you are thinking of". I complied with his request.

"You are thinking of a violet". I admitted I was.

"Now look at the paper in your pocket". On it was written the word Violet. "How do you do it?" I asked.

"I read your forehead", he replied simply, as though that explained everything. All this was done, of course, to impress me. And I was suitably impressed.

"All right", I said. "Now tell me the other things I should know, including the date of my demobilisation".

"Ek rupee", he said, and I handed him a rupee. He thought for a few seconds before replying.

"You will have some good news on the 22nd November". This was followed by rather irrelevant scraps of information, like a bald headed man with a small moustache would help me in business and that the initials of three people who would help me were M.P.H.

He also advised me not to give away secrets that other persons could profit by.

I made a mental note of the date November 22nd, and asked him outright. "Now tell me the date when I shall leave India to be demobilised".

He thought for quite a time before replying. "Sometimes you like India and sometimes you don't. But when you leave India you will not return". This was interesting as I was due for a posting to Ceylon. If I was never to return to India, it could mean that I would be demobilised from Ceylon.

"What about my demob date?" I reminded him.

Again he paused before replying.

"You will leave India on March 2nd or 7th next year and will not return".

I thanked him for the information and he 'salaamed' me and mingled with the passers by. After he had gone I made a note in my diary of the dates mentioned, not altogether convinced that he could know the date of my demob, as at that time even the powers-that-be didn't know.

Eagerly I awaited for anything that could possibly be classed as 'good news'. Oh, and on that day my posting to Ceylon was cancelled which I didn't think was good news at all, but on reflection it may have speeded up my demob date.

Three months later I was due for two weeks hill leave to which I was looking forward. All arrangements had been made, and on February 21st I was just boarding the lorry to the station, there to catch the midnight train to Calcutta when the Admin. Officer dashed up and I heard my name called.

"That's me, sir" I said. "Is anything wrong?"

"Your demobilisation notice has just come through and you are not to proceed on hill leave. You must get cleared and be at Worli on March 1st."

I was dumbfounded. It was very disappointing being deprived of my hill leave, but I was glad to know that I was to be demobbed shortly.

"Can't it wait a fortnight, sir?" I asked.

"Afraid not. You've got to start right away with your with your clearance papers. Report to the Admin Office in the morning". So

I climbed down from the lorry, my kit was taken off, and I said goodbye to my friends who were going on leave.

In due course my clearance was completed and I made the long train journey to Bombay where I arrived on March 2nd. There followed a few days in which I was inoculated, my kit handed in, currency changed, and endless parades, and on March 7th I boarded the ship for home. And as the shores of India receded I recalled the words of the Indian fortune teller, told me a year previously. "You will leave India on the 2nd or 7th of March next year and will not return"

GO WEST

Cowboys, Indians, buffaloes, and the Mounties. As a boy I was thrilled by the tales of the Wild West, of the great cattle ranches and round-ups, of Indians in buckskin jackets and trousers, feathered head- dresses and moccasins, riding the Great Plains and hunting the buffalo; of the Mounties in their scarlet tunics, cowboy hats and blue trousers with a yellow stripe down the seams, who kept law and order in the wilds of North-west Canada.

But it was not until late in life that I achieved my boyhood ambition of going out West to see for myself the Indians and the prairies, the cowboys and the cattle ranches. And I was not disappointed.

The West is still there, not so wild, but still colourful, and the romance lingers on. There are vast cattle ranches in Alberta and British Columbia, with cowboys rounding up the cattle much as they used to. There are many Indians who take a pride in their history, and who can be seen in the glory of beaded buckskin and feathered head-dress at their regular powwows, at stampedes, or on "Indian Days", when they dress in buckskin jackets and trousers and magnificent feathered head- dresses; and live in teepees like their forefathers did.

Herds of buffalo, once nearly extinct, are again on the increase, and a limited amount of hunting is allowed, which provide the Indians with food, skins and robes.

At the hotel in which I stayed at Banff in the Rockies, they had a Bighorn Lounge with a wide open brick fireplace containing huge burning logs which cast a warm glow on the redwood panelling of the room. A cowboy coming into the hotel, in a ten-gallon Stetson, lilac shirt, faded jeans and high-heeled boots, raised no attention, neither did a Mountie when he came in, although there was some speculation as to what he had come for.

The roads in the town are named after animals: Beaver Street, Caribou Street, Elk Street, etc. The street signposts are of gnarled tree trunks, with hand carved wooden signs indicating the names of the streets.

Many of the cabins and bungalows are of timber and clapboard, and the tangy smell of woodsmoke lingers in the fresh mountain air I saw my first Indian family in the Indian Trading Post where they come to bring their tanned skins and beadwork for sale. They were Stoneys from the Morley Reservation, about forty miles away. They were dressed in cowboy hats, checked shirts, store trousers, and moccasins.

The head of the family was named Wild Man and spoke fairly good English; but his companion, a hawk-nosed savage looking buck, his squaw and two children apparently spoke no English. I asked for permission to photograph them outside the store, and after a consultation in their own tongue, they agreed, a dollar helping to dispel any reluctance.

Through the good offices of a cowboy, with whom I had been out riding, I was introduced to an Indian chief and his family, in full ceremonial costume. The Chief wore a fine white buckskin jacket beautifully decorated with beadwork; buckskin trousers with fringes down the sides, and a magnificent head-dress of eagle feathers which descended to his beaded moccasins.

He was chief of a Stoney Band who lived on the Morley Reservation where the Indians raise cattle, do some haymaking, tan skins for making jackets and other handicrafts for sale. The women do the beadwork and quill work on the tanned skins.

The Chief was well over 70 years of age, and told me that in his younger days he acted as an interpreter for the Government and was given a small pension. Every July, the Indians from the Reservation dress in their finery, and make the journey to Banff, where they set up their teepees and for a week live the life they used to, holding shooting contests, running races, horse races, and dancing to the sound of tomtoms, bone rattles, and whistles. Many of these Indians still keep up their old time ceremonies and traditions and elect their own chiefs, who are recognised by the Government.

Yes, the romance of the West lingers on, and many tour operators are now arranging tours to the West. With the rate of exchange being so favourable, now is the time to Go West, and enjoy a unique and romantic holiday.

Hymns

Suggested tune. St Peter (CM).   A.Reinagle 1799-1877
Hymn 13 Standard Edition A & M.
As now the sun's declining rays

It was two thousand years ago
Our Lord was born on earth.
His mother was a lowly maid
Who gave this wondrous birth.

In boyhood he knew discipline
As well as joys and tears.
But he was destined to be wise
Beyond his early years.

He lived a life so good and true
That even in his day
He changed the lives and souls of men
And taught them how to pray.

He did not boast, or shout, or rave.
He taught them to be meek.
To fight the angry, not with blows
But turn the other cheek.

His teachings were not popular
With those in high estate.
They seized him on a trumped up charge
And led him to his fate.

He suffered death upon the Cross
To purge our sins away
And now with thankful hearts we sing
Our hymn of praise today.

About the Author

Percy Barsby was an accomplished author, poet and painter.

Percy spent his entire life in Long Eaton, Derbyshire and Attenborough, Nottinghamshire apart from two years in India during World War II. He was very involved with many village organisations.

Percy was devoted to his wife Mabel and their four children.

A devout Christian, Percy was very active in his local church, including serving in the choir for over 80 years and the Parochial Church Council for over 60 years.

Percy had over 4,400 articles published in over 80 periodicals. His paintings were exhibited in England and France including the Royal Institute Summer Salon.

Percy had a life-long fascination with Gypsies and North American Indians.

Colophon

The book is printed in Times New Roman font, predominantly 12pt. Spacing between some lines in the poems has been modified to ensure best fit. Paragraph spacing is a multiple of 1.15 to allow for easy reading.

The art work on the front page was digitally altered to remove a small water spot and some rust stains.

www.ingramcontent.com/pod-product-compliance
Lightning Source LLC
Chambersburg PA
CBHW060805120626
46557CB00001B/99